CW00448709

Cruise

A Blayze Carlson Novel, Volume 1

Zak Yates

Published by ZPY Publications, 2020.

CRUISE
A Blayze Carlson Novel

First edition. September 2nd, 2020.

ISBN: 9798666389157

Dedication

This book is dedicated to our eight-month-old kitten, Blaze, who sadly passed away while I was writing it.

PROLOGUE

On a warm, dark, rainy night in the middle of September, blue and red lights lit up the runway at Orlando International Airport. The case that the FBI had been working on for almost two years had gone stale, so they had brought in Special Agent Blayze Carlson from the New York office, as he had a reputation for closing cases quickly. It hadn't taken long for him to catch his man, the international drug lord, Manuel Rudzinski, who had evaded capture for years.

Blayze's new boss in Orlando, Assistant Director Stone, came over to congratulate him. "Well done, Special Agent Carlson. I heard you were good, but not this good." She reached out her hand and he reciprocated.

"Thank you ma'am. It's all about teamwork."

"Well, they couldn't have done it without your help. This is one of the biggest results the Orlando FBI team has seen in years, and it's all thanks to you, Blayze."

Rudzinski was not only wanted for the distribution of Class A drugs all over the world, but also for the murder of five people of various nationalities. He had been due to fly out to Europe that evening, but Blayze had intercepted the flight details and caught him just before he took off. They found ten million dollars' worth of cocaine on his plane and arrested three other men from his gang. Once Manuel and his men were in custody, and the police cars had dispersed, Assistant Director Stone called Blayze back over. "So I suppose you'll be heading back to New York now this is over?" she asked.

"Well, I was thinking of taking a brief vacation while I'm down this way. I fancy the Caribbean."

"I recommend Antigua," she said. "Its beaches are exquisite."

"Last time I was on a cruise it was for work. This time I'd like to soak up the sun and relax."

"Well, you've earned it after this."

They headed back towards the Assistant Director's car and Blayze opened the door and let her in. As he closed it she wound down her window. "After your cruise, how would you feel about staying down here with us for a while? We could do with someone like you on our team."

"Can I think about it while I'm away and let you know when I return?"

"Of course you can. Enjoy your trip." The car pulled away, leaving Blayze standing there with an empty plane behind him and his car just a few yards away. He was the first man on the scene and the last man to leave. Just how he liked it.

The next morning, sitting in the temporary apartment that the bureau had found for him while he was there to help on the case, Blayze searched online for a cruise. He had been to most places before, so fancied a change. Remembering what his boss had said, he found one that, although it had more sea days than ports to visit, had places he hadn't been to before. Antigua and St Lucia. They looked beautiful in the pictures on the website, and a day lying on the beach was just what he had on his mind. He didn't mind the sea days as that was his time to relax, with a nice cold beer in hand and a vast open ocean between him and work. Every ship he had been on before had a gym, so he'd have a quick workout in the morning to keep fit, then sunbathe in the afternoon to tan his muscular body. What more could you want from a vacation?

CHAPTER ONE

Blayze had not been on this ship before, the Majestic Dream, but he had travelled with the same cruise company, Paradise Cruises, and knew that some things would probably be the same. This ship was a lot bigger than the previous ones he had sailed on, as he soon came to see when he arrived at the dock. It loomed over the pier building that he was about to enter, to join the queue for boarding. The large windows of the outside cabins were lit up by the sun shining on them, making the ship look radiant, and the royal blue writing of the ship's name made it seem grand and elegant. The queue moved quickly and Blayze headed up the gangway, the ship becoming bigger and bigger the closer he got.

The vast atrium that greeted him as he stepped on the ship was five decks high and had a large chandelier hanging down from the ceiling above, secured by attachments so it didn't move. He was given a map of the ship by one of the staff as he passed by security after checking in, so he knew where to go.

He walked a little further in, so he didn't block the entrance, and placed his large rucksack, the only piece of luggage he had brought with him, on the ground behind a couple of seats that had people in them. Glancing around, he could see people all over, already perusing what the ship had to offer. There was a mixture of age groups on board, ranging from young families with their babies to the occasional old couple who looked like cruise aficionados.

Opening the little map, he saw that there were so many venues and things to do that he didn't know if he would even have time to visit them all. There was a theatre, a shopping mall, two sports lounges, a piano bar, comedy lounge, jazz bar, gym, spa, indoor pool and outdoor pool, rock climbing, golf, basketball court, splash park, various restaurants serving a variety of cuisines, and a casino. Although not all of those interested him, he wanted to check out the gym and rock climbing. The casino was also on his list of places to see during the cruise, as he liked a good gamble, but only when he was on vacation. When on land, he hardly went out, as the job came first and he would spend hours and hours on cases, not really having time for a social life.

That was the biggest reason that Blayze was cruising alone. He had been single for almost five years, ever since he'd gotten promoted to Special Agent. He had focussed more on work than he had on his relationship and, one night after closing a case, he went home to find his girlfriend had left him. He loved his job too much and knew that it would come first, before anything else. Being single had made him free to move around the country wherever the bureau needed him, as he had no ties.

The first stop, though, was to find his cabin and get unpacked before going for a little stroll around to familiarise himself with his new surroundings for the week. He picked up his bag and set off to Deck 6. Cabin 6050 was the number on his booking form, which was only one deck up from where he was. He walked up the stairs and followed the arrows, directing him to his cabin. He had requested an outside cabin as he wanted a window to see where he was and to enjoy the view along the way. He opened his door and found a large double bed with a TV on the opposite wall. There was a bedside table at either side of the bed, each with a little lamp on, and a chest of drawers next to the double wardrobe. Alongside the drawers was a desk which had a set of stationery laid out on top and a chair tucked underneath.

He dumped his bag on the floor by the bed and went to have a look at the bathroom. A simple toilet, sink and shower, but that was all that he needed and it had all the amenities in it, so he didn't have to buy anything. From cruising before, he knew that he would have a cabin steward who would be in twice a day to make the bed, leave fresh towels and take away any rubbish. He didn't have to lift a finger for a whole seven days, which is what he was looking forward to. Now he had checked out his cabin and dumped his bag, it was time to explore the ship and see what it had to offer.

IT WAS THREE-THIRTY and the ship's horn had just blown, signalling the soon departure from the port of Miami. For Simon, this was just another seven-day cruise around the Caribbean, and seven days closer to the end of his contract, which was only a month away. It wasn't his turn to work embarkation or debarkation today, so he had spent most of the morning in bed and had popped into Walmart to buy some snacks for his cabin just after lunch. He enjoyed sail away and always popped up to the bow of the ship, where only crew members were allowed, for a cigarette and to sit and watch Miami fade into the distance. Although the deck wasn't massive, and certainly would not fit all of the crew on it at the same time, it still had room for sun loungers around a small empty pool, which Simon had never seen filled ever since he had arrived. Behind a screen, were tables and chairs for people to sit and smoke at, covered from the wind and rain. Attached to the edge of the bow on both sides were lifeboats that were covered up ready to be deployed if ever needed.

As the ship pulled away from the port and started heading towards the open ocean, Simon looked through the gaps that the ropes went through and could see that dolphins had joined them, swimming alongside the ship. More crew had joined at this point and had scattered themselves across the deck, and as Simon looked back up towards the bridge, he noticed a crowd of new guests had appeared, leaning over the railings above. The random waves from guests, who had already been drinking since they came on board, made him feel like he was in a zoo. There were only a few places on the ship that were out of bounds to the passengers, and the bow was one of them. It was adjacent to the crew bar and one of the few smoking areas for the crew. You could be yourself there and not have to put on a fake smile, although you still had to wear your name tag at all times, which told everyone your job and which country you were from.

Laughs came bursting out through the door from the crew bar — the only entrance to the bow — which made Simon turn around. It was Laura, Rachel and Andrew, some of his cast members, dressed in their evening uniform and looking smart, as they had just finished doing embarkation duty. The entire entertainment department got on so well that during their time on board they had become like a family. He moved closer to them, now smiling from their infectious laughter as they made their way to a table near the doorway. Andrew noticed Simon and waved. "You should have seen them, Simon. You missed a right laugh there."

"Hey, guys. Come on, what happened?" Simon replied eagerly as he reached the table and took a seat.

"This couple were running late and were rushing to get on board," Laura started. "As soon as they set foot on the ship, the guy dropped his bag by his feet and stopped. His girlfriend bumped right into the back of him and pushed him over his bag. He fell to the ground, and she landed on top of him."

"Oh my God, no way," Simon said with a chuckle and a surprised look on his face.

"The crowd of people, who were getting their drinks in from the bar, just roared with laughter, and started clapping as the couple got up. It was the funniest thing ever," Rachel added.

As Simon put out his cigarette, he looked at everyone still laughing. "How embarrassing."

"The guy just stood up and waved at everyone, but the girl put on her sunglasses and kept her head down. She couldn't wait to get out of there," explained Laura.

"Best way to end the four hours of embark, though." Simon reached in his pocket for another cigarette.

Laura and Rachel stood. "Right, we're off to get out of this uniform and get some of this glorious sun before tea," Laura said as they made their way to the exit.

Simon and Andrew stayed sat down and waved to the girls as they left.

"You done much today?" asked Andrew.

"Same old shit, really. Slept in for a change, Walmart, and now here. Off to do next week's weekly duties soon so you guys can put your swaps in by tomorrow," Simon replied.

"Cool," Andrew said, nodding his head. "Listen, I'll leave you to it and get out of this uniform myself. It's too hot with this jacket and tie on. Catch you later." Andrew stood up and left, leaving Simon sitting on his own.

Still with half a cigarette to go, Simon stood up and made his way back to the bow of the ship. The water was so calm that it was only the ship's movement causing any waves. The breeze that was now on Simon's face was from the ship getting faster, and it was a welcome relief. There had been no wind all day, which had made him sweat while just standing still. As he looked out across the large open ocean that was in front of him, he noticed the distant ships ahead that had left the port before them. He thought to himself that he wouldn't get that view again for a while, knowing his contract was nearly up and that this would be one of his last times. Twelve years he had been dancing on the ocean waves, and it was time to give the sea legs a break and move back to the UK to settle on land.

Simon stood there, looking out ahead for an hour, and then realised he still had the duties rota to get done, so he headed back inside, down the three flights of stairs to the crew quarters area. Walking down the main corridor, known as the I95, he passed the dancers' area and grabbed last week's rota, which was still up on the notice board. While he was there, he tidied the board, as there were too many old notices up from previous events that had already been and gone.

He headed back to his cabin, which was further down the ship, just off the I95, and sat at his desk. As he waited for the computer to load, he peered out of his porthole as the water splashed up against it, thinking about how lucky he was to have a window. The other dancers had shared cabins with bunk beds and a bathroom, and when the light went out, it was complete darkness. Being the dance captain, Simon got his own cabin with a double bed and a view. Small luxuries, but luxuries nonetheless. Simon's duties were to maintain the production show's standards by holding weekly rehearsals and re-blocking the staging if anyone became injured or sick. He also produced the duties rota as the dancers performed extra duties each cruise, assisting the rest of the entertainment team.

The screen loaded, and it didn't take long to rotate people along and print out the new rota, which he took straight down to the dancers' notice board and then returned to his room to relax before tea. The dancers had a show on the first night, but Simon wasn't in it, so he didn't need to have tea early. He just had to watch it and take notes to make sure everything was okay and there were no issues.

After the show had finished, Simon was in the crew bar with a Bud Light in hand, waiting for any of the dancers to walk in. He knew some would definitely turn up as they never missed a drink before bed, while others who were not drinkers wouldn't. They would only go out during the monthly crew parties that were always some sort of themed event. Andrew appeared and headed straight to the bar. Without even asking, he turned up to the table where Simon was sitting and handed him another Bud Light.

"Cheers, hun," Simon said, raising the bottle he already had in his hand and nodding his head.

Andrew sat next to him, wearing the tightest of vest tops, showing his skinny physique, and some tiny shorts. He loved showing off his legs, especially at the crew parties, when his alter ego, Miss Monthly, would come out of the closet. "No worries, lovely," he replied. "What are we doing in rehearsals tomorrow?"

"Not much to do, to be honest, with only a month to go. I may just give everyone the afternoon off."

"What's happened to you?" Andrew asked in shock. "Are you getting soft in your old age or something? Or is it you have a new boyfriend you're not telling me about?"

"Cheeky bastard! I'm only a couple of years older than you," Simon said, smacking Andrew on the arm. "And no, it's certainly not a new boyfriend. After that last one, I need a break from relationships."

No one else turned up, which surprised Simon, but it didn't matter as he didn't want to be out too late. He made a quick call to Laura in her cabin and asked her to put a note up saying 'No rehearsal tomorrow' on the notice board and to pass the word onto the others. Simon and Andrew both sat and had one more drink each before heading off to bed.

With it being a full day at sea the next day, Simon checked to see if he any morning duties himself, which he didn't. Having just cancelled rehearsals, he poured himself a large vodka and diet coke and lay in bed to watch a film, as he could have a nice long lie in.

The moonlight shone through his porthole, and the television was still on as Simon woke up. It was only two-thirty in the morning, but the need to go the toilet outweighed the need to sleep. In a dazed state, Simon looked out of his porthole. It didn't look as though they were moving at all. The sea had been calm earlier, so he thought nothing of it and, after visiting the toilet, he turned off the television and got back into bed.

BLAYZE HAD BEEN ON many cruises in the past, some for work and some for pleasure, but his favourite thing about them was the peaceful nights. There was something about being in the middle of the ocean he found calming and relaxing and he tried to get on a cruise, that wasn't work related, at least once a year to have time to himself. When on vacation, Blayze would get up early every morning to go to the gym before anyone else got in there. He would have something to eat and then find a nice quiet spot to catch some sun, before heading in for a siesta so he could enjoy his time alone on the top deck, just him and his bucket of beer, once everyone else had gone to bed.

He lay on a sun lounger under the stars with just the added glow from festoon lights that ran the length of the ship. There was no one else around, and the silence was just what he had wanted. He was dressed in Hawaiian style shorts, a white short-sleeved shirt which was unbuttoned halfway down, showing his pecs and the top of his abs, and flip-flops. It was a warm evening and there was no breeze at all. This was because the ship had stopped moving. Initially, this hadn't phased him, as it wasn't the first time a ship he had been on had stopped in the middle of the ocean. The times before were engine issues, or picking up a handful of Cuban men, who were trying to get to America on a raft, but those times were always during the day. He'd never known a ship to stop in the middle of the night before. This made him question what could have happened. As someone whose job it was to get answers, he finished the last beer in his bucket and walked around the top deck to search for anything which would assist his quizzical mind. Every few yards he stopped and leaned over the balcony to peer down below to see if he could spot anything, but it was quiet.

Having walked around for some time, Blayze was just about to turn in for the night when he heard his name called out from behind him. He quickly turned around as he wasn't expecting anyone he knew to be on board. There stood Ananda, the chief security officer.

"Hey, man," Blayze called out, recognising him right away.

"When I saw your name on the passenger list, I knew you'd be out here somewhere at this time of night."

"Ananda! Bloody hell, great to see you." They walked towards each other and exchanged a handshake and a brief hug.

"You too, you too. Been a while, my friend."

"It certainly has. How long have you been on here for, then?" Blayze asked as he moved towards the rail close-by to lean against. Ananda joined, and they both looked out at the darkness in front of them, gazing at the stars above.

"Six months almost. Two more to go and then I get to see my family."

"Are they keeping well?"

"Yes, yes. All good," Ananda replied with a smile. "Is it work or play this time?" he asked.

Turning around with his back now to the railing, leaning back on both arms and looking extremely chilled, Blayze replied, "Very much play this time. Thank God. Feet up under the stars with a bucket of beer and who knows, maybe a pretty girl or two along the way."

"Well, man, you enjoy, and I'm sure I'll catch you again soon. I've got to do my rounds, but great to see you," Ananda said, as he pushed himself up from the railing.

"Before you go, can I ask why we've stopped?"

"I'm not entirely sure. We will know more in the morning."

Ananda walked away. "Cheers, man, you have a good night," Blayze said as he waved him off.

Making his way back down to his cabin, Blayze thought it best to unpack, as he had just chucked his rucksack down on the floor by his bed. He put his clothes in the wardrobe and chest of drawers and sat on his bed. It was late, but he was still hungry and he knew that room service would still be available, as it was a 24-hour service. He looked at the menu that was on his desk, and noticed they did his favourite sandwich, the Monte Cristo with ham, crunchy on the outside and tender in the centre. He phoned to order one, knowing it was just what he needed to soak up those few beers he had earlier. The food arrived quickly, but that didn't surprise him as at nearly three-fifteen he knew he would have been one of just a handful of people that would still be awake. Cutting open his sandwich and seeing the cheese ooze out from the centre made his mouth water, so he tucked straight in. Food eaten, it was time for Blayze to get his head down. He wanted to be up at six and in the gym so he would be ready and focussed for the afternoon of gambling he had planned.

CHAPTER TWO

Simon woke up early because of the sun beaming through his porthole. The lie in he had wanted didn't happen, so he got out of bed and into the shower. When he got back into his room, still drying himself off, he headed straight for the porthole to see if what he had seen in the middle of the night was still the case. And it was. The ship was motionless, just sat there. It was like they had docked there for the night, which they had never done before. The ocean was calm and picturesque, and the sun glistened over the tiniest of ripples.

He sat at his desk and powered up his computer so he could check his work emails like he did every morning in case there were any changes to the day ahead. He wanted to see if there was any news about what was going on and why they were not moving. Once it had loaded, he noticed he had quite a few unread emails, but there was one from Antonio, the staff captain, labelled 'IMPORTANT', asking all the heads of department to join him in a meeting in his office at nine o'clock sharp. It was still only six-thirty, so Simon had plenty of time, and yet the message seemed urgent. It was a good job he had woken up early, he thought, otherwise he would have missed the meeting. The only emails Simon used to get from Antonio were ones for unacceptable behaviour. They weren't regular emails, but he had had to take two of his dancers up to Antonio's office at the start of their contract for having a cabin party until the early hours of the morning, even after security had told them to stop. Luckily, because they were new to ships, they got off with a warning.

It was still too early to call Robert, the cruise director, to find out if he knew what was going on. As with any full sea day, it was to be a long day ahead for all the cruise staff on board, with a host of activities planned to keep the guests happy and entertained. In fact, it was a long day for all the crew members on board, as the bars and restaurants would be busy with many hungry mouths to feed. A full cruise, which this was, meant that there were 3525 passengers on board and 1598 crew members. After going through the rest of the unopened emails that he had received overnight, he deleted most of them as they were not important to him and just generic 'send to all' emails, which he hated getting. He got dressed in his cruise staff uniform and was ready for his usual morning routine.

Grabbing a cup of coffee from the crew mess hall, which consisted of two coffee stations, a juice machine, hot and cold buffet style food, a cleaning station, and many tables and chairs, he took it up to the crew deck. He was ready for his first cigarette of the day. On the open deck at that time of the morning, very few people were about. It was a warm morning, but not too hot. Just how Simon liked it. The sky was clear with not a cloud in sight, and there was no breeze at all. The sea was tranquil, perfectly still, looking like a sheet of blue glass. Two cabin stewards arrived on the deck shortly after Simon, ready in their uniform for their morning rounds. Simon waved to acknowledge them and they waved back, but it was too early for conversation, so Simon turned away and kept drinking his coffee, lighting another cigarette. A black coffee and two cigarettes was Simon's breakfast. It was what he called a dancer's diet. Not that he needed to diet at all; he was in great shape for his age. At thirty-two, he could still perform just as well as he did when he was twenty, which his cast admired. The only things that gave away his age were the odd grey hairs that kept appearing and the occasional aches he sometimes felt. Nothing a good massage in the spa didn't cure.

The door opened to the crew deck and out walked Robert. Simon waved to call him over.

"Morning, Simon. You're up early," he said as he sat in the chair opposite him. "Did you wet the bed again?"

"Swimming in it, as usual," Simon joked back. "Hey, what's with the email from Antonio?"

"I'm not sure, to be honest. We're in the same boat, pardon the pun. I felt the ship starting to slow down last night, but no one has given me any answers yet. I've been awake since one o'clock and I can't get back to sleep."

"I saw we weren't moving when I got up to pee, but I was that knackered, I fell straight back to sleep."

"Must be something," Robert said, "they normally tell me everything straight away."

"Well, I was going to ring you when I read the email this morning, but I know what a sea day is like for you and thought you'd be asleep."

"Wish I had been. I need to know as soon as possible before guests start asking questions. I hate not being able to give an answer. Even if it's a little white lie to divert them, at least it's something. I'm in the dark here."

Andrew appeared in the doorway looking a little worse for wear, hair all over the place like he'd just rolled out of bed. Usually he was extremely well groomed, and wouldn't be seen dead in public looking anything but immaculate.

"Bloody hell, look at the state of you," Simon said, staring right at Andrew's hair, which was pointing in different directions. "Who dragged you through a hedge backwards?"

"Don't ask. He booted me out this morning for farting on him. Well, that was what he said. I don't remember doing anything at all."

Simon and Robert looked at each other and burst into laughter.

"Fuck off, you bastards!" Andrew said as he pulled up a chair and joined them. "He just can't handle my beautiful aroma, obviously."

"We all know your aroma after a few beers, mate," Robert added. "Cleared an entire section of the crew party once, if my memory serves me correctly."

"That was the curry night too, though, it always does that to me. It just slipped out," Andrew replied.

"I bet it did," Simon said with a smirk on his face, followed by a slap on the arm from Andrew.

Andrew looked around and looked confused as he noticed the stillness and the lack of movement. "Hang on a minute, have I missed a couple of days or something? Why aren't we moving?"

"Erm, we don't quite know, we're finding out soon," Simon replied while looking at Robert to see if he would say anything.

"I hope we haven't broken down. I've got an excursion planned in Antigua and I've been waiting ages for it. Got to do it now before the new cast come on as it will be non-stop rehearsals."

"Don't worry. We've a meeting soon to find out what the problem is and then we can let you all know," Simon replied to Andrew. He looked at Robert, who had stood. "See you up there shortly."

"Catch you guys in a bit," Robert replied as he pushed his chair under the table and walked away.

Andrew watched as Robert walked through the door and then turned back to Simon. "He's up bloody early, isn't he, for a sea day?"

"So are you."

"Had no bloody choice, love. He pushed me that hard that I fell out of the bed and onto the floor. Thank fuck we weren't in my bed, otherwise I would have fallen off the top bunk." Andrew was dating the male singer who had his own cabin with a double bed, near to Simon's cabin. "I will catch up on sleep later when he's in the gym."

"Good plan. Like I said, we don't know what's going on, but you know what it's like, we'll get the brunt of it and have to come up with some extra duties to help keep the passengers occupied."

"True that, but please, I beg you, babe, don't put me on ping pong duty if you have to add anything, I fucking hate that shit." Andrew put out his cigarette and walked towards the door. As he reached it, he turned back to Simon. "Let us know what's happening after your meeting, boss."

"Will do," Simon replied, waving his hand to say goodbye.

Still having some time to ponder what the meeting was all about, Simon went back downstairs for another coffee. Knowing this could turn into an even longer day than normal, he needed extra fuel. While down there, he decided he should break his routine and get some breakfast. The thought of food instantly made his stomach rumble. As he walked into the crew mess hall, he bumped into two of his dancers, Tammy and John. "Hey, you two, up early aren't you?" he asked. "Why is everyone up so early today? What's happened?"

"Dude, don't ask," John replied. "We've been hooked on the series '24' and we've only got four episodes left. As soon as we saw your sign for no rehearsals, we thought, why the hell not try to finish the box set off? We need something to eat before we finish."

"It's been a long night, and we ran out of snacks hours ago," Tammy added.

"Fucking hell, you two. I don't know how you do it," Simon said while following them into the queue by the food counter.

"Give me one night with Kiefer Sutherland any day," Tammy added, taking a plate from the top of the pile.

"Well," said John, who grabbed a plate and pushed past her. "We all know you like it rough and within a time limit, but twenty-four hours, really? More like twenty-four seconds."

"You cheeky fucking bastard!" she snapped, slapping him around the back of the head.

Simon and John started laughing as they knew the reputation Tammy had for having a quick one now and again, and when they said a quick one, they meant, 'wham, bam, thank you ma'am'. Simon didn't know what her secret was, but somehow she could make a guy orgasm on cue. It was like she clicked her fingers and there it was.

They sat down, ate their breakfast, and talked about various scenes from '24', with Tammy and John trying not to give too much away as Simon hadn't seen it all yet.

"Shit, it's ten to nine. I need to go," Simon said after having a glance at his watch. "See you both later." He jumped up and took his plate to the trays near the door, putting his plate in one and his cutlery in another; it was something every crew member had to do to help out the kitchen staff. He headed to the elevator and pressed the button. He watched as the numbers got lower and lower, finally reaching his level. He got in and hit the button for Deck 9, where Antonio's office was situated. It was time to find out was going on.

BLAYZE WOKE UP AT SIX o'clock and freshened himself up before getting his gym gear on. Wearing a pair of black shorts, a tight black vest top, trainers and his gym gloves, he grabbed a water bottle out of his fridge, took his mp3 player out of his case and headed upstairs for his morning workout.

As he entered the gym, it was just how he liked it: empty. He was the only one there, so could do whatever he wanted. He had a brief walk around to see what equipment this ship had, as it seemed much bigger than the last ship he had been on. The windows were facing the front of the ship and arced around the entire gym, bringing in the morning sunlight. He hopped on a treadmill that was by the windows and did his warm-up on there. Putting his headphones in, he flicked through his music and found his rock anthems. "Perfect," he said. He pressed play and started the machine. As he looked out ahead it felt like he was walking on the ocean. He was only on there for fifteen minutes as he wasn't much of a cardio lover, but he knew he had to keep it up for work. No good chasing after suspects and having to give up because you're out of breath.

After finishing his warm-up, Blayze headed over to the free weights section of the gym. There were five benches to choose from, so he took the middle one in order to be central in the mirrors in front of him. Before starting, he lifted up his vest to check out his abs in the mirror. He had an eight-pack and a well-designed V-shaped body that he had been working on every morning for the past three years. Knowing his days in the office could be long and tiring, he always did his gym workouts in the morning beforehand, as they gave him the energy to last him the rest of the day. After doing his chest workout on the bench, he stood close to the mirror and moved onto his arm workout, watching his muscles grow with each repetition.

Two ladies entered just as he was finishing his last set and made their way towards the bikes that were next to the row of treadmills he had been on before. He noticed them staring at him as they walked past and just smiled back at them.

The last part of his workout was his weighted squats, which he knew would grab the girls' attention. He moved away from the wall so that they could get a splendid view of his buttocks as he squatted. It worked. Every time he went down, he looked into the mirror towards their direction and caught them watching him. He honestly thought one of them was bound to fall off her bike at some point, so he stopped and finished, taking one last look at his body in the mirror, then headed back to his cabin.

After a nice long shower, Blayze went up to the Lido deck for some breakfast. He didn't want a lot to eat after just finishing his workout, so grabbed some fruit and some orange

juice and headed to his quiet spot that he had found the previous night to get some sun. It was already hot, and it hadn't
even turned 8:30 yet. The spot he had found was unfortunately
not as quiet as it was late at night, and more and more people
turned up as the morning went on. He lay there for a while
soaking up the morning sun, but as the surrounding noise got
louder and louder, he decided it was time to head back in.
Putting his top back on, he headed to the gift shop. He didn't
want to buy anything; he just wanted to have a look around to
see what they had. He was killing time until the casino opened
as he had already planned his day ahead.

THE ELEVATOR OPENED and Simon could see a crowd of
people standing outside the staff captain's office, awaiting the
nine o'clock meeting that he had scheduled. Robert emerged
out of his cabin, which was on the same deck, just a few doors
down from Antonio's office. He gestured for Simon to come
and stand by him. All the heads of department were there, as
per the staff captain's request, plus he had also invited a few
more staff members who held senior positions. As soon as the
clock struck nine, Antonio's door opened, letting the crew in.

　　The room quickly became crowded as it was not a large office. It only had enough room for a desk, two chairs and a filing
cabinet. The staff captain was sitting behind his desk and waited for everyone to enter. The chief engineer and safety officer
both took a seat in front of him. The food and beverage manager, staff engineer, environmental officer, chief security officer,
hotel director, and doctor stood close together against the wall,

leaving just enough room for Robert and Simon to squeeze in. They closed the door behind them.

"Good morning, everyone," Antonio began.

As people started saying good morning back, all Simon could think of was how nice the Italian accent was, remembering an old boyfriend he had from there many years back.

"Sorry to squeeze you all in here, but this is the only place that no one can hear what I have to say." Taking a deep breath and looking around at the inquisitive faces before him, he continued. "I'll get straight to the point. The captain is missing."

Everyone in the room looked at each other in disbelief at the news, and the whispers got louder as people tried to work out what he had just said. Robert looked at Simon. "Holy shit. Missing."

Antonio gestured for the chatter to die down so he could carry on. "He was due to be on board the bridge last night at 22:00 for his last checks, yet he never showed. They called me to the bridge after the officers could not reach the captain in his cabin or on his mobile. So as not to alert anyone, I did all the checks myself, and told them I would check on the captain after I had finished, which I did, but there was no answer then, either."

"He was okay at eight o'clock, as we had a cigarette together on his balcony," the chief engineer added.

Antonio noted the time mentioned on a piece of paper in front of him. "I've been awake all night searching the ship myself from top to bottom and there is no sign of him at all. I stopped the ship in case of the worst scenario." People in the room looked at one another. "I've called his number every ten minutes, in case I had missed him while searching, but unfortunately there has been no answer every time. I wanted to wait until now to say anything in case he turned up, and if not, to see if any of you could shed some light on his whereabouts." Antonio gazed around at the faces in his office who just looked blankly back at him, with some just shaking their heads.

"No one?" he asked. "Right. Here is the plan I have come up with. No one outside of this room is to know what is going on. As far as anyone is concerned, the captain is in his room suffering from a back injury, and I will take over for the time being. Everything must look normal to the crew and passengers, but I want every one of you here to search every section of your respective area every two hours, and report back to me with an update. Keep your eyes and ears open and report anything. I will make an announcement to tell the crew that there has been a malfunction in the engine room and that it is being fixed and we should be on our way shortly." He turned to the staff engineer. "Make something up and get them to inspect things."

Turning back to address the entire room, Antonio carried on with his plan. "To make the search easier for everyone, I will move up the scheduled bomb drill to 11:00 today so we can get a look in all the crew's cabins while they are searching too, not knowing that this time the bomb is actually Captain Argenti. Is this clear?" He was met with silent nods from all. "Okay, thank you, everyone, and like I said, this is between us for now." As they all made their way out of the office, Antonio shouted, "Robert, just one moment, please." Robert stayed where he was and Simon waited in the doorway.

"Listen, Robert," Antonio started. "I want you to make all of today's announcements to the passengers. They will want consistency and you are just the man. You will be the face of this, so add in as many distractions as necessary and we will get through this."

"No problem, sir, will do," Robert replied and left the office, closing the door behind him.

CHAPTER THREE

Simon followed Robert into his cabin. They walked down a small hallway which lead past a door to the bathroom and another to a bedroom. As they turned the corner they entered Robert's open plan living room and office. Before they both sat down, Simon asked, "What the fuck was that about?" Simon took a seat on the couch near the window and Robert sat at his desk, both silent, trying to process the meeting they had just left.

Robert pulled off the daily 'What's On' sheet, which got delivered to every cabin the night before, from his notice board and laid it out in front of him. It listed every activity that was to happen throughout the day in all areas of the ship. He grabbed a highlighter out of the top drawer of his desk and highlighted a few events. "Give me two minutes, mate, I need to do this morning's announcement."

"Yeah, no worries," Simon replied. He sat back on the sofa and turned to look out of the patio windows that Robert had. Admiring the stillness and peacefulness that was out there, Simon sat and listened to what Robert had to say.

Robert coughed to clear his throat and then pressed the button on his intercom. He paused for a couple of seconds as he had to wait for the 'ding dong' to have sounded before he could speak. "This is your cruise director, Rob, here and a very good morning, ladies and gentlemen, boys and girls. Welcome to your very first day at sea on board the Majestic Dream. As you may have noticed we are currently not moving. Please do not worry as we are making some necessary checks and will set sail again soon. We have lots of things to do today, including ice carving on the Lido deck at ten, followed by a salsa dance class with one of our very talented dancers, then once you've worked those hips, you can relax with a general knowledge quiz, hosted by your lovely assistant cruise director, Alice. If you're feeling lucky, the casino opens in fifteen minute's time and, if you haven't done so already, get those shore excursions booked for the wonderful ports of Antigua and St Lucia as there are so many things to do and see. We have various activities planned for you throughout the day, so make sure you have a look in your 'What's On' guide. Tonight, we have the first of our fabulous Vegas-style shows in the main theatre, located at the front of the ship, which you don't want to miss. Whatever you decide to do, we will see you out there soon. Have a wonderful day." He released his finger and paused again, waiting for the 'ding dong' to finish. He swivelled around in his chair to face Simon. "All done."

Simon turned away from the window to face Robert. "What do you think about the captain, then?"

"I'm not sure, but we need to get out there today and distract people, while also searching."

"Lucky I cancelled rehearsals, hey? I've got some extra time on my hands now, so whatever needs doing, I'll do it. Changing the subject: where was David this morning?"

"I tried calling him, but I presume he had a few drinks last night and passed out. He's always missed morning meetings though, sending some sort of excuse afterwards. He'd make them all if they were in the crew bar from 7pm onwards."

"Very true," Simon snickered.

"Listen, Simon, you can't tell anyone about what is going on."

"I know, I know."

"I'm serious."

"I know, and I'm sorry about last time. I didn't mean to let it slip that I saw Tammy leave your cabin that one time. I wouldn't have thought anything of it except she winked and wagged her little finger as she passed me." Simon mimed the actions as he spoke. "It just came out one night after plenty of booze."

"Thanks for the reminder and fuck off," he replied, noticing what Simon's actions insinuated.

"Anyway," Simon continued. "That was months ago, and no one has mentioned it since, so I think you're safe." Simon stood up and headed towards the cabin door. "I need to let the dancers know about the bomb search being moved up in case they decide to get their bodies out on show for the officers on the bridge, like they usually do on that crew deck."

"Okay, yeah, brilliant. I'll inform the hosts and band, but everything, and I mean everything, must run smoothly today."

"No problem, boss, I'm on it." Simon saluted like a sailor as he left the cabin, closing the door behind him.

BLAYZE WAS ON HIS WAY to the casino after grabbing a bite to eat from the sushi bar. He had made a promise to himself that he would only ever gamble on a cruise, and never on land. After watching his brother take regular monthly trips to Vegas a few years ago, nearly losing his house and family, he never wanted to be in the same position. Even though Blayze was single, his apartment, back in New York, meant everything to him. His bachelor pad had everything he had ever wanted in it, and he had worked hard enough not to lose it. This was the only time he would do it, and he had set a little money aside just for this occasion.

He reached the casino floor and looked around, noticing there were empty seats at most tables. Lights were flashing all around the walls which were covered with slot machines and, as there wasn't a dress code, the sight of flesh was prominent from those having a quick gamble before heading outside to be in the sun. His favourite game was blackjack, and he headed straight there. Blayze sat down and said hello to everyone, ready to play, but he wasn't there for friendship. He was there to make money. He handed over his first hundred dollars, and the croupier passed him his chips. He sat there for almost two hours, winning some hands and losing others, but after a good few hands he was finally up by eighty bucks, which he was happy about.

Not wanting to lose his winnings, he decided it was time for a change. He looked around at the other tables and noticed that the casino had suddenly become busy. With the ship still not moving, many people had made their way inside, looking hot and flustered, fanning themselves with their 'What's On' guides. The need for the ship's air conditioning had become apparent, especially since there was no breeze outside to cool people down.

While waiting for a spot on another table to open up, Blayze made his way to the bar and perched on a stool at the far end, trying to stay away from as many people as possible. The last thing he wanted was for people to know what he did for a living and have them treat him differently for the rest of the week, which had happened on vacations in the past. It was easier to stay away. If anyone asked, he would lie. He had created a story on a previous vacation that he worked in sales and the more times he told the story, the better the lie became.

"Can I get a Bud Light, please?" he asked as the bartender approached.

"Of course, sir," came the reply, and within seconds, she had placed one down in front of him. "Would you like a glass with that?" the girl behind the bar asked.

"No thanks, I'm good," Blayze responded, then took a great long sip, enjoying the refreshing taste.

"Drinking already?" Blayze heard from behind him, but he recognised the voice.

Blayze placed his beer back down on the bar and lifted both hands up in the air. "Ananda, you caught me." He swivelled round, dropping his hands, and shook Ananda's outstretched hand. "Still not moving, I see," he stated, turning his attention to the long stretch of windows nearby.

"They are working on it as we speak," Ananda replied. "You go ahead," he said to the security guard that he was with. "I'll catch you up." He turned back to Blayze and leaned on the bar. "So, are you winning, then?"

"So-so, for now, anyway, but I've not got started yet. Maybe this will help," raising his Bud Light in the air.

"I'm sure a couple more and you'll be fully there."

"Only a couple for me at this time, I'm not a big day drinker. Hey, is the captain okay? I've not heard him making his usual announcements," asked Blayze, taking another swig. Having been on ships before, he knew that the captain normally gave a daily report over the tannoy.

Ananda looked to his left and right and could see the bar was very busy. "He's, eh, got a bad back and is resting in bed. Nothing to worry about."

His look and hesitant reply didn't sit well with Blayze. "Ananda, what's up?" He could see right through people. It was part of the job, and he could tell that his friend was lying to him.

Ananda tapped the bar and pushed himself away. "Don't worry, you just think about winning. Listen, I have to go, but I'm sure I'll catch you later on my rounds." He quickly turned and walked away, not waiting for any response.

Blayze sat there for a few moments, pondering what Ananda had said, and questioned why his friend would lie to him like that. As he looked on he noticed a spot had opened up on a Texas Hold 'em table and he wasn't going to miss the opportunity to grab that seat and try to make more money. Leaving the last dregs of his beer on the bar, he rushed over, forgetting what had just happened.

A few hours went by and it was only because of the rumbling of his belly that he looked at his watch and realised it was time to get ready for his dinner seating. Happy enough that he had turned his winnings from $80 to $450, he cashed his chips out and headed back to his cabin. As he made his way down the stairs, he passed a security officer doing her rounds. He suddenly remembered how Ananda had reacted when he mentioned the captain earlier. He would need to find him later to ask him what was going on.

THE MORNING HAD QUICKLY passed and Simon was back in his cabin having a brief rest before it was time to get ready for his afternoon bingo duties. The search for the captain had continued throughout the day, but they still had not found him. The morning's bomb search had gone as planned and had produced nothing except hangovers from three musicians, who had, by the look of them, been up most of the night having a party. They had been rudely awoken by Simon and Robert banging on their door for a cabin inspection. The day's activities, conducted either by the dancers or the hosts, went ahead with no issues at all, just as Robert had instructed. No questions about the captain or why the ship hadn't moved were asked by anyone, so Antonio's plan of distraction had been working until Simon received a phone call from Rachel.

"Hey, sweetie," she started. "You haven't seen Captain Argenti, have you?"

"Not today," he responded, wondering why she would be looking for him. "What do you need him for? Is there anything I can help with?" he asked.

"It's a personal matter, hun, so I doubt it."

"Oh, not him too?" Simon replied, referring to her quick and easy ways. He understood exactly what she had meant by the word 'personal'.

"He's been a regular since I got on board, sweetie. You know me, a sucker for the older guys."

"A sucker of most guys," he replied with a chuckle.

"No need for that now. Anyway, if you see him, tell him I've been looking for him."

"Will do, hun, see you later." He hung up the phone and immediately called Robert.

"What's up?" Robert asked straightaway. "Any news?"

"We may have a problem. Rachel has been asking if I've seen the captain today. Apparently he's a regular of hers, if you get my drift, and she will only continue asking when she doesn't hear from him."

A few moments of pause happened between them as they pondered how they could defuse the situation, then Simon piped back up.

"I tell you what, I'll ask her to do my bingo this afternoon, which will keep her busy, especially as it's a seven-game one, and then she'll go for her afternoon nap before show time. How does that sound?"

"Brilliant idea, yes."

"I'll just say that you need me for something, planning the cast handover week's schedule, or something like that."

"Excellent. I'll leave that with you."

Simon quickly got back on the phone to Rachel and asked her to cover his afternoon activities, which she didn't mind doing. She was always offering to cover people's bingo sessions as she loved to play the host and call out the numbers. Everyone used to mock her and say that she had missed her calling in life, and that the day she retired she would have to get a job at a bingo hall.

The plan was working. He just hoped that she wouldn't start asking the others she was working with, as he didn't know who else knew about the two of them being a regular thing. Captain Argenti was married and had three kids who lived back in Italy. They had recently been on the ship for three weeks for a family visit, not long after Rachel had got on. His wife knew that he had another woman on the ship; he had one on every ship he worked on, so this one wasn't any different. The age old saying 'What happens on the ship stays on the ship' was a motto of Rachel's. She had already caused issues on some of her previous ships, and had broken up a couple of marriages, so she wasn't shy of a drama or two.

Now with the rest of the afternoon off, Simon put his feet up on the bed and turned the TV on when there was a knock at the door. He shouted, "Come in," and David entered the room, still looking a little rough from the night before.

"Late night, was it?" Simon asked. "I could hear you guys through the wall."

"Mate, don't," David responded, shaking his head while making his way to sit on the edge of Simon's bed. "Whose idea was it to invite the Russians to a cabin party?" he asked himself. "Jesus, they can drink. Anyway, Rob's asked me to pop in, as he was busy when I called, to get a heads-up as to what happened at that stupid o'clock meeting."

"You musicians are like bloody vampires. Asleep all day and up all night," Simon joked, looking at David's pale face, which was partially hidden by his curly black hair that ran to his shoulders. Simon went into the full details of everything that Antonio had said, and what the plan was that he had come up with.

"Wow, okay, no captain. Where the hell could he be?" David asked, with a puzzled look on his face.

"That's the problem, no one knows anything. We're not to tell anyone; we just have to say that he's injured and leave it at that. A missing captain all over the news? They would have a field day."

"True that. Anything you need from me?" David asked, knowing that he'd missed most of the day's searching already.

"Just keep an eye out really, but as we've got the show tonight, we will be busy, anyway."

"Cool, no worries. Will do." David walked out and then turned back. "You out tonight?"

"It's show night, isn't it? I'm always out."

"Cool. Catch ya later." David exited and closed the door behind him.

After a brief rest, and squeezing in an episode of '24', it was time to grab something to eat. Once he returned from the crew mess hall, it was time for a shower and shave, so he was ready to head upstairs to get ready for the evening's show. Tonight was the first of their main Vegas-style shows they performed every cruise and it required a big physical warm-up beforehand. As he made his way up the stairs towards the backstage area, Rachel caught up with him.

"Hey, sweetie, still not heard from him, you know."

"Maybe he's just busy with the ship still not moving."

"Oh yeah, I had completely forgotten about that. Will make the show nice and easy tonight." She was moving quicker than Simon and was now a few steps ahead.

"This is very true. It will make a nice change to actually lift you in the air and not have to worry which way the ship is rocking. See you up there soon." Simon watched as she ran up ahead of him. Once she was a flight above, he let out an enormous sigh of relief.

"What's up with you?" Andrew questioned, sneaking up behind him.

"Don't fucking do that! You'll give me a heart attack," Simon shouted back.

"Alright, jumpy, calm down or your blood pressure will go through the roof."

"Oh, shut up and run up those stairs, you could do with the extra exercise," Simon remarked while aiming his eye-line down at Andrew's waist. There was absolutely no fat on Andrew's body at all, and yet he always thought he was fat and hated anyone who mentioned his weight. It was the biggest reason he was in the gym on the treadmill every day.

"You're a twat, you know that?" Andrew replied, throwing his middle finger up in Simon's face as he ran up the stairs past him.

"You love me, really!" Simon shouted up after him.

"You fucking wish," came the reply, which echoed down the metal staircase.

With a chuckle to himself, Simon carried on up and reached backstage.

BLAYZE QUEUED UP OUTSIDE the dining hall, waiting to be let in. There were many people already waiting with some dressed in their finest outfits. Blayze hadn't brought his suit with him but had on a white shirt that had vibrant colours splashed all over it, which fitted his body perfectly, a pair of skinny black jeans and his dress shoes. As the doors opened, they were all shown where to sit. The Maître D' showed Blayze to his table as they had put him on the Captain's Table for that evening's dinner. It quite surprised Blayze as he had never been on the Captain's Table before, and wondered if Ananda had pulled some strings.

As he sat down he was met by a newly married couple, who were sitting directly to his right, and a mother and daughter to his left. They exchanged pleasantries and talked about the various things they had been up to that day. Blayze turned to see the rest of the dining room. It was enormous and was split over two levels with a grand staircase that spiralled, joining the two floors together. Most of the tables were large round ones which hosted several cabins per table, but there were also some smaller ones dotted around for the more intimate dinners. As he looked around, he noticed some officers walking towards them and turned back to the table. "The captain's on his way," he said to his dining companions for the night. As the officers approached the table, they all stood up to shake their hands. Blayze noticed their name tags and read them all. Fabio, the chief engineer, Donato, the safety officer, and Antonio, the staff captain, had joined them. They all took their seats and were immediately handed a menu from the waitstaff who had been awaiting their arrival.

Once everyone had ordered, Antonio introduced himself and his staff to the guests at the table.

"Excuse me, sir, but is the captain not joining us tonight?" the elderly mother to his left asked.

"I'm really sorry, but the captain is not feeling very well tonight and is having to give engagements a miss," Antonio responded.

Starters arrived, and the conversation halted while they all ate. As soon as Blayze had finished, he asked, "So can I ask what the matter is with the captain?"

"It's nothing, really," Antonio began. "He has injured his back and has been advised by the ship's doctor to rest it for a couple of days. Nothing to worry about."

"I had a bad back too, once," stated the girl to his right. "I couldn't walk for days."

This sparked off all the other guests on the table reminiscing about their lifelong ailments, which didn't interest Blayze at all. He turned to the nearest waiter and asked for another large glass of red wine. He noticed that the two other officers with the staff captain were very quiet and hadn't said a word to the table since the initial hello when they had walked in. They only ever uttered a few words in Italian to each other between courses, which followed with them leaving for a cigarette out on the deck.

The meal went by with more stories of people's pasts, which bored Blayze. He couldn't wait to get out of there. He wasn't a people person, and small talk was not his thing. As soon as they had collected the dessert plates, Blayze stood up and said his thanks before leaving the dining room. He headed straight for the nearest bar and ordered a large whisky on the rocks. He sat on the bar stool, knocked it back, and instantly felt calmer. He had planned to go and see the show that was on in the main theatre for a bit of escapism, but because he'd just had to sit through people talking all the time, he didn't want to be around anyone else. He ordered his bucket of beer and headed back to his cabin for a while, knowing that as soon as it hit ten o'clock he could make his way up to his spot and relax again under the stars.

THE SHOW HAD GONE NICE and smoothly, with no issues, and had received an enthusiastic reception from the audience, who had given a standing ovation. Once the costumes were hung up and the dressing rooms were tidy, it was time for a few drinks in the crew bar. Most of the entertainment department, along with a host of crew members from other departments, were dotted around the bar, chatting away and listening to the music that was playing in the background.

As Simon entered, he grabbed a drink and headed straight out onto the open deck for a cigarette. After the shows, the dancers usually met outside, as long as the weather was okay, to get some fresh air and cool down. One by one they came outside and joined Simon around the table, talking about how nice it was to do that show without the ship moving. Everyone except Rachel had shown up. They stayed and chatted for a while, but knowing that there was still another sea day ahead before reaching their first port of call, people weren't drinking their usual amounts. Some of them had to be up first thing as duties started early the next morning and some activities were no fun with a hangover.

Time sped by and it had just passed one in the morning when Simon knew he had to hit the sack. Leaving just a few people there who he had been talking with, he headed back down towards his cabin. He heard someone on the phone at the bottom of the staircase, which caused him to slow down. It sounded like a heated argument and, as Simon got closer, he recognised the voice. It was Rachel. She heard him coming and shouted, "Fucking bastard!" down the line, then hung up the phone. She stormed off down the corridor, not saying a word. Simon tried to catch her, but it was too late as she had quickly nipped down the dancers' corridor and locked herself in her room. Not knowing if Lisa, her cabin-mate, was in or not, he left it and went back to his room. He was tired and needed to sleep. After getting up so early, finding out the captain was missing and searching for him, planning extra duties, doing a bomb search and finally doing a show, Simon was exhausted. Hoping for a lie in and an easier day tomorrow, Simon shut the catch to his porthole to darken the room and got into bed.

CHAPTER FOUR

Simon woke up early again, this time not because of the sun, but from the sound of the waves crashing against the side of the ship. They were obviously trying to catch up on the time lost, as the ship was travelling at speed, causing it to bounce on the waves. After getting himself dressed, Simon headed upstairs for his morning routine — a coffee and a cigarette — and as soon as he stepped outside, the reason for the bouncing became apparent. The wind was powerful and there were large swells in the ocean as he glanced ahead, the complete opposite of what it had been the previous day. That kind of weather didn't bother him, though, as he was used to it at that time of year. Hurricane season was one of Simon's favourite times to be on board; he enjoyed a good storm and the motion the ship made as it rode the waves. He loved watching people's faces who had experienced nothing like it before. The look of terror as they thought they were on the Titanic and it was the end always amused him.

"Storm's a-brewing, I see," said a voice behind him. As Simon turned around, he noticed Robert had made his way to one of the tables in the shelter. They were the only two outside.

"Morning, Rob," Simon said, making his way to sit with him. "Heard anything yet?"

"Absolutely nothing, mate. Kinda worrying, really, as it's been over twenty-four hours now and no one has seen or heard from him at all." He took a sip of his coffee and leaned forward on the table, holding his flask with both hands. "If we don't find him soon, we must notify the police and coastguard of a missing person."

"How can a person just vanish like that and no one see anything?" Simon asked, lighting up his cigarette, now sheltered from the wind.

"I don't know, mate, it's a weird one." Sitting back in his chair, Robert let out a long yawn. "It's gonna be a long day today and I've not had much sleep, yet again. With this weather, there's gonna be a lot of sick passengers around. No doubt the odd one will try to get a full refund for his cruise because the weather has ruined his experience."

"There's always one, isn't there," Simon agreed.

"We will probably need to move a few of the activities inside today so watch out for updates throughout the morning and let your guys know of any changes, if that's okay? I'll email you once I've had a chance to move things around."

"No problem. I'm sure once they get up they will understand and know why."

"Right. I need something to eat before cracking on," Robert said while standing up, and Rachel appeared at the door. "Morning, Rachel, you're up early," he noted, as no one ever saw her before nine unless she had to be up for something.

"Couldn't sleep," she started, as she made her way towards the table. "I'm worried about Captain Argenti. He never misses our meet-ups. He's always particular about the time and place."

Simon remembered seeing her shouting at someone on the phone the night before. "Was it him you were shouting at last night on the phone for missing your little get-together? I tried to catch you, but you were too quick."

Simon gestured with his eyes to Robert to sit back down and listen to what Rachel was saying. He took a seat and lit up another cigarette.

"No. That was another dickhead who can fuck right off. Jealous bastard, that's all."

"They are the worst, aren't they?" Robert added and looked directly at Simon, raising his eyebrows, awaiting the same look back. The 'are you thinking what I'm thinking' expression was a little too obvious and Rachel had also spotted it.

"What's going on?" she asked hastily.

"Nothing, don't worry," Robert replied quickly.

Simon knew they couldn't tell the captain's mistress what was going on, as that would make the situation ten times worse.

"Obviously it's not nothing, with the look on both your faces. If that fucker has done anything, I swear to God, I'll chop his fucking balls off." She stormed off with rage, clearly upset.

Simon and Robert sat there for a moment, waiting until Rachel had gone and they heard the door close.

"You don't think it's a jealousy thing from an ex-lover, do you?" Simon asked.

"It's something to consider," Robert replied, tilting his head with a pondering expression on his face.

"Jesus, we'd be looking all day, she's got that many. Could be a crew member, or even a passenger. You'd have to print her picture on the back of the 'What's On' guide, with the heading 'Have you slept with this girl? If so, call this number.'"

"Could you imagine her face?" Robert replied. After a brief pause he continued. "We'd be the ones having our balls chopped off."

Crossing his legs at the thought of that happening, Simon replied, "Yeah, maybe not the best way to find out who she was on about. I'll try to catch her later when she's a little less stressed."

"Good idea. We could definitely do with finding out who she was on about." Robert stood back up and headed towards the door. "Let me know later if you get to find out who it was. I'm off for that breakfast I wanted half an hour ago."

Simon sat there, wondering who it could be that she was talking to on the phone. Going over the names of the dancers alone, she'd probably had most of them. Some girls, too, he had heard, but he could rule them out as her comments were heavily male-orientated. The amount of guys he had already heard about from her made the list of potentials long enough, let alone the other hundreds of male crew members that would need to be deducted. If it was a jealousy thing, he thought, no one normally goes missing. The odd fight, maybe, but to go missing is a totally different ball game.

Now feeling hungry himself, Simon made his way down the stairs to the crew mess. The smell of the food when he got there made his belly rumble even more, but all he fancied was some scrambled eggs on toast. Grabbing another cup of coffee, he sat there, alone, eating his breakfast. After he had finished, he headed back to his cabin to find out what duties Rachel had on for that day, and what the best place would be to catch her off-guard to get the answers he was after.

SITTING IN HIS OFFICE, Antonio heard a knock at the door. "Come in," he shouted, and the door opened. It was his chief of security, Ananda, and he gestured to him to sit down.

"Sir, we've searched everywhere multiple times and still no sign of the captain. What is the next step?"

Antonio paused for a second and let out a deep breath. "We need to contact the coastguard and the police, as we now have a missing person on our hands," he explained. "We also need to let the crew know what is going on. I will email all the heads of department now and organise a full crew meeting for eleven o'clock tonight in the main theatre. That will give me time today to contact the authorities and find out what they want us to do."

"Good plan, sir." Ananda suddenly remembered who was on board. "Let me make a quick phone call." Ananda made his call while Antonio began typing his email. "Sir, I have someone on their way up to meet you who could help us. I will wait for them by the stairs and bring them in, if that's okay?" he asked.

"Yes, of course," Antonio said. He had always trusted Ananda's judgement.

After he had finished his email, Antonio waited for Ananda's return. A couple of minutes passed by, then a knock came on his door. "Come in," he shouted. In walked Ananda, followed by a man. Antonio stood up and offered his hand.

"Good morning, sir," the man said.

"Good morning," Antonio reciprocated. He wondered how he recognised him. Then it hit him. "It's you from the Captain's Table last night."

"Staff captain, let me introduce Special Agent Blayze Carlson, FBI."

"FBI. That was quick, I've not even called them," remarked Antonio, sitting back down. He gestured for them both to take a seat across from him.

"I'm actually on vacation, sir, but I knew something was up. I've worked with Ananda before on a different ship, when I was undercover, and I could tell he wasn't telling me everything when I saw him yesterday in the casino. What's the issue?" Blayze crossed his legs and leaned back in his seat.

"Well, Mr Carlson," Antonio started.

"Please," he interrupted. "Call me Blayze."

"Okay, Blayze, we have a situation. Captain Argenti has gone missing, and we have not seen him since around ten o'clock on Sunday night. That is why the ship wasn't moving yesterday. We needed to search everywhere, inside and outside the ship. I held off starting the engines for as long as I could, so as not to arouse suspicion, but we had to start moving this morning or too many questions would have been asked. Only senior officers and heads of department know, and they have been searching night and day."

"Who was the last person to see him?"

"The chief engineer left the captain's cabin at eight o'clock and he was due on the bridge at ten o'clock, but he never showed," Ananda reported. "Something happened within those two hours, but we don't know what."

"Have you contacted the coastguard?" asked Blayze.

"I am about to do that now, and then call the Miami police department," replied Antonio.

"I will contact the FBI to let them know the situation and tell them I am helping you on board. Can I take a look at the captain's quarters to see if there is any evidence of foul play? We can't rule anything out at this time."

"Of course. Ananda, please escort Blayze to the captain's cabin. If there is anything you need, please contact me by dialling 7791 from any phone on board. I have scheduled a meeting with all the crew at eleven o'clock tonight in the main theatre, if you would be so kind to be there? I can introduce you to them and reassure them we are doing everything we can. We have to tell them the situation in case any rumours begin."

"Yes, of course," Blayze responded as he stood up, reaching out.

"Thank you," replied Antonio, shaking his hand.

ANANDA LEAD BLAYZE down the corridor to the captain's cabin, which was right next to the door to the bridge. As Blayze entered, he looked around the first room he came to for any signs of a struggle. Nothing seemed out of place. He walked around the lounge and office, checking the drawers at his desk before making his way to the bedroom. He looked through his bedside drawers and wardrobes, yet it did not look as though they had been touched. While searching them, Blayze found that the captain's wallet was in the top drawer by his bed, with money still inside. He had also noticed earlier that there had been some money out on his desk, too. He ruled out a robbery straight away, as they would be the first to go. He went and sat at the captain's desk and, with a shuffle of the computer mouse, the screen came on, which revealed his emails. He had not logged off, so presumably had not intended to leave his cabin that night. Blayze sat down and read through the emails that had been sent and received around the time of his disappearance. There didn't seem to be anything out of the ordinary. No one asking to meet up, no threats, nothing. It was like he had disappeared into thin air.

"No one has asked any of the crew about the captain yet, have they?" Blayze asked Ananda, who was standing near the door, not wanting to get in the way.

"Not yet. The staff captain didn't want to alert anyone yet, in case he showed up."

"Okay, so I'll ask tonight at the meeting after he's made his announcements."

"My team will help you with whatever you need."

"Cheers, Ananda. Okay. I need to speak to the chief engineer to ask what they were talking about and find out the captain's frame of mind."

"I'll call him now and find out where he is."

"Thanks," Blayze replied as he took one last glance around the room. He spotted a family photo on his desk and looked right at the captain. "Where are you?"

They left the captain's cabin and headed down to the engine room to talk to the chief engineer.

HAVING SEEN THAT RACHEL would be on library duty between three and four in the afternoon, Simon thought that would be the best place to ask her about who she was arguing with, as she was not allowed to shout or swear in guest areas. It was just after lunchtime and he had already done his search around all of his designated areas, looking for the captain who had now been missing for nearly forty hours. He had received an email from Antonio to say that they had reported the missing captain to the coastguard and police and that there was to be a full crew meeting at eleven o'clock for all updates. Antonio still wanted them to keep checking, just in case they had missed anything.

Simon sat on his bed and pressed play on his DVD player. He was in the middle of watching series three of '24', trying to catch up with the rest of the cast so they didn't spoil it for him. It helped to pass the time on long sea days and gave him something different to talk to the cast about instead of just work all the time. He had only been watching for fifteen minutes when "OSCAR, OSCAR, OSCAR" came bellowing through the PA system in his cabin. This was followed by three prolonged blasts on the ship's whistle. "Shit, not again," Simon said to himself out loud. He jumped off the bed and put his shoes back on and rushed out of the door.

It had only been two weeks since the same code and alarm had sounded, when a passenger had fallen overboard in the middle of the night, having partied too much. The crew knew the drill all too well and rushed to their positions to help. The officers manning the helm knew the Williamson Turn well and had already steered the ship to the port side. This time, though, it was the middle of the day, so it would be much easier to track the person who had gone over the side of the ship.

The swells in the ocean were gigantic because of the high winds, so as Simon reached the port side to help keep a lookout for the person bobbing up and down between the waves, he was met with shouts of "There they are," "Where have they gone?" and "There they are again." This was a pattern that kept repeating over and over by everyone around and, because it was still early in the day, it had attracted the attention of many passengers, overly eager to help but mostly just getting in the way. At this point no one knew who it was that had gone overboard, as they were too busy monitoring the last place they had pointed at, which kept moving further away as the ship made its manoeuvres. This distressed some passengers who were standing right by Simon.

"Why are we moving further away? Why are we leaving them?" cried a middle-aged woman, worried about the situation, but not worried enough for her to leave her cocktail behind to help.

"Sorry, miss, but would you mind stepping back from the railing? We will be turning sharply soon to head back for them," Simon replied, trying to usher the lady back from her front-row seat of the action.

"Well, I won't be able to see then, will I?" she said after sipping at her cocktail.

"And we won't need to point at someone else if you end up over too now, will we?" That was a reply she did not accept well, and, with shock on her face, she retreated back towards the wall. It was that type of passenger that got on Simon's nerves, but he never normally said anything, except in situations like this when it was about life and death.

The wind was powerful, and the ship was struggling in the rough waters. It was taking a little longer to get back to their original position than it had done two weeks earlier. That night, though, the sea had been much calmer with no wind, so the extra time it was taking did not surprise the crew at all. Simon had called Robert to ask him to make an announcement, asking all passengers to remain off the decks due to the high winds and rough seas, which he did, yet it didn't stop some of them trying to get a good glimpse of the action.

As soon as the boat got near the spot, the engines were stopped, enabling the release of the rescue boat. Watching it try to ride the huge swells reminded Simon of a rollercoaster. It would climb up and up, then disappear out of sight, keeping everyone on edge, hoping it would appear again.

It seemed like ages before the boat found the body, but then, in the distance, Simon could see something being pulled up out of the water and onto the vessel. It raced back as fast as it could, bouncing high on the waves. There was nothing more Simon could do, as the person overboard had been safely rescued. He knew that once on board they would be with the medical team and have plenty of people around them.

He headed back down to his cabin to continue watching his DVD. When he got back, he saw that the DVD player had rudely turned itself off and hadn't saved where he was up to. He tried to remember at which exact point he was, but for the life of him he couldn't, so he just turned it off and headed for a coffee instead, waiting for the time to pass by until he could speak to Rachel in the library.

BLAYZE AND ANANDA WERE on their way towards the engine room to talk to the chief engineer when the 'Bravo' siren sounded. "Blayze, I've got to go, I need to get to my post," said Ananda, turning back around and heading up the stairs.

"I'm coming with you," Blayze said, following in pursuit. They reached the I95, the major hub of the crew quarters which ran the length of the ship, and headed towards the stern, stopping by the ship's loading dock. Blayze noticed that some cages, which had carried passengers' luggage on board, were still erect in the corner. Ananda's security team had all gathered in the same position, awaiting orders.

"What do we do?" Blayze asked.

"If they find someone, we need to open the door respective to where they are and collect the body from the rescue boat, assisting the medical team if necessary."

They listened on their radios so they could hear what was going on outside. They couldn't see anything yet as they kept the door closed until it was needed; this stopped any water splashing unnecessarily into the ship. It seemed like they were standing there doing nothing for ages doing nothing while a person was potentially drowning out there. But every crew member had their part to play, and Blayze knew that this was their job.

After a short while, they received the news that a body had been rescued and that the lifeboat was on its way back to the ship. Ananda gave the order to open the side door. As soon as the door opened they were met by a wave of water splashing up against the side of the ship. Blayze looked out and saw up close that the waves were powerful, and that this rescue was still not over. They still had to transport the body from a moving lifeboat onto the ship without causing further harm.

The lifeboat came into view and the security team took their positions, making sure that they were secured to the ship so they did not fall into the ocean themselves. The boat pulled up alongside the ship and attempted to get close. With its first attempt, the lifeboat crashed into the side of the ship, which knocked two of Ananda's guards to the ground. Quickly getting up, they resumed their positions, ready for the next attempt. This time they were able to get close enough to get hold of the body and lift it onto the ship.

The medical team rushed in with a stretcher and lifted the body. As they passed Blayze, he could see that the casualty was female, but he also noticed the amount of blood all over her face. Not something you usually see from a fall, he thought as he watched them take her away. He also noticed that she had a name badge on, so he knew then that she was a crew member, but they moved her so quickly that he didn't have time to read what it said. Blayze stayed to help Ananda and his guards shut the door and put everything away.

"Appreciate your help," Ananda said.

"Well, it's not every day I get to do something like that. Do you know who it was?" he asked, looking back in the direction the stretcher had been taken.

"By the name badge, she must be crew, but I couldn't tell who. Looks like there were some facial injuries, though. Maybe she hit something on her way down."

"I will head down there shortly to find out, as you never know. I need to get changed first, though. I can taste the salt from the sea water all over me." Blayze headed back to his cabin to get changed, but he couldn't get the image of the girl he had just seen out of his mind. He needed to know who she was, and how she had sustained those injuries.

CHAPTER FIVE

With the rescue boat now back in its position, the ship's engines started up, and they were back on their way to their first port of call, Antigua. The bars and restaurants had reopened, along with the casino, which had many people waiting to recommence the games they had been in the middle of when the alarms had sounded. With the reassurance from the cruise director over the tannoy system, the ship had gone back to its normal hustle and bustle and the drinks had begun to flow. Before it was time for Simon to head to the library, he decided to have a walk across the Lido deck to make sure all the activities on the schedule were happening.

He walked past the ping pong table, which was tucked into a corner at the front of the ship, sheltered from the wind, and noticed John standing there keeping score, as two junior kids tried to outdo each other. It looked very intense, each with their own crowds behind them shouting encouragement. Passing by an over-crowded bar, he looked across, past the stage, and saw a line of people queueing at the burger counter.

Laura was on the stage setting herself up for the afternoon's dance class, which had already attracted a lot of attention, as it was country-themed. She was wearing black cowboy boots and a short denim skirt, and she had tied her shirt up under her boobs, making them more prominent. This had attracted some adolescent boys, all huddled together, leaning against the side of the Jacuzzi which was behind two rows of sun loungers, watching her every move. They were obviously not there to dance, but just to whistle while she did. Simon waved, and Laura waved back with an enormous grin. She always made herself look presentable and wanted men to look at her wherever she went, hence her boobs always being on show. Simon knew, though, after having many deep conversations with her, that she was quite an insecure person and that it was all a show to give her confidence. He kept moving towards the stern of the ship where the library was situated, just a few decks below him.

As he reached the large main pool in the centre of the ship, he nodded and waved at some passengers who had caught his eye, avoiding stopping and talking to them in case they interrogated him for more information about the person who was rescued. Reaching the end of the deck, after passing another two bars full of passengers, he looked at his watch, which said 2:45. He was still a little early, but Simon thought he would head down anyway and just sit in there, quietly waiting.

The library only hosted a few chairs and tables which looked out onto the ocean. The adjacent wall had locked cabinets all the way down it, out of which guests could sign books and games during scheduled library hours. After waiting for twenty minutes, the time had come and gone for when Rachel should have started her duty, so he called down to her cabin, but got no answer. He waited a little longer and still there was no sign of her. Knowing the library needed attending, he stayed, taking every chance he could to call her. Luckily, Simon had a spare key to the cabinets on his keyring and was able to open them all.

Simon had now covered her duty for thirty minutes when his phone rang, and it was the doctor. An unusual call, Simon thought, as the doctor hardly ever called him. The only time he called was when a dancer had wanted to do the show, but he had told them they needed more rest, and had called ahead in case they had tried to put a spin on it. Every other time he just received an email, and he knew that none of the dancers were off injured. The call was brief and Simon was just asked to make his way to the infirmary as soon as possible. Eager to find out why, he closed the library early as no one was in it, and headed downstairs. Thoughts flashed through his head of an injured dancer, causing him to wonder if he would have to re-space the entire show — that they were to perform in just a few hours — for an injured dancer. As he reached the door to the infirmary, Robert was waiting for him.

"Did they call you, too?" asked Simon.

"Yeah, but they haven't said why yet," replied Robert as he opened the door, letting Simon in first.

As they entered, the nurse, who was sitting behind the desk, greeted them. She had been told to expect them and without them having to say anything she said, "I'll get the doctor for you," and headed through a door behind her. She returned just a few moments later. "You can go through now." She held the door open, letting them both past.

"Thank you," said Robert as the nurse closed the door.

"Have a seat, both of you," the doctor said, gesturing to the two armchairs on the opposite side of his desk. As they sat, the doctor continued. "Unfortunately, I have some dreadful news."

Simon and Robert turned and looked at each other to see if anything sprung to mind, then turned their attention back to the doctor who was leaning forward with his arms on the desk, looking slightly down.

"We were able to identify the person who was rescued from the sea earlier. Although she had a name tag on, we still had to formally identify the body due to the injuries caused to the face. Unfortunately, there was nothing we could do for her as the injuries she had sustained had caused severe damage, which I can only presume occurred before she went overboard."

The pair glanced at each other again, still having no idea who he was talking about.

"I'm really sorry to have to tell you both this, but the deceased is Rachel Lawson."

Simon looked at Robert, then back at the doctor. "This can't be right, you've made a mistake."

"I'm sorry, but we have double-checked everything. It was Rachel Lawson who was recovered from the sea. She was pronounced dead shortly after arriving here." The doctor made his way around to Simon's side, placing a hand on his shoulder.

Simon burst into tears, and Robert put his hand on his leg in an attempt to comfort him.

"I can't believe it," Robert uttered, shaking his head.

"I'll give you guys a couple of minutes alone," the doctor said, then exited the room.

They sat there for a few moments, not saying a word, just trying to comprehend what the doctor had just said. Only the occasional sob from Simon broke the silence in the air.

"I need to tell the cast," Simon managed to get out.

"I need to let the family know, first, then I will inform the staff captain that there will be no show tonight," Robert said. "There is no way I can let you all go on stage after finding out something like this. You need to be there to support each oth-er. I will make an announcement, saying we have technical is-sues, or something like that, once everyone has been informed." Robert got up from his chair and went to open the door to let the doctor know they were ready.

Rubbing his eyes, Simon stood up and composed himself as he now had to let everyone know. "Thanks, Doctor." With a shake of the doctor's hand, he left. Simon phoned Laura, as he knew by looking at the time that she would be back from her class. He asked her to knock on everyone's doors and tell them to head backstage in fifteen minute's time, no questions asked, and that it was imperative that everyone be there, including the dancers, singers, musicians, and technical crew. This gave Si-mon just enough time to head upstairs for a smoke and to gath-er his thoughts, and to figure out how he would break the news and appear to be the strong one.

AFTER HEARING THE NEWS that the rescued girl had died, Blayze had asked to see the body. He wanted to learn more about the injuries he had seen when they had rescued her. He was standing next to the body with the doctor, who pulled back the sheet to reveal Rachel's face.

"We have tried to clean her up as best we can, but her in-juries were severe," the doctor said. Blayze took a closer look. "You will notice that she has a broken nose and bruising to both eyes. When washing her, we could feel that her jaw was broken, and that she was also missing three of her front teeth.

She has a gash down her scalp, which is why there was so much blood on her face."

"Could these injuries have been caused by a fall?" Blayze asked.

"She would have had to hit something very large on her way down, and with an enormous impact, to cause injuries like these."

"Were there any other marks on her body?"

"She has some bruising to her wrists and to her left side."

"Potential signs of being grabbed and punched," Blayze stated.

"Yes, they could be."

"Any signs of sexual activity?"

"None that would suggest forceful entry, if that is what you're asking."

"Thank you, Doctor, I've seen all I need to."

As Blayze left the room, he called Ananda, asking him to meet him on the top deck on the port side, where Rachel had been seen falling overboard. He got into the nearest elevator and headed straight there. As soon as he arrived, he began looking over the balcony for any clues as to what may have happened.

"Blayze, how can I help you?" Ananda asked as he approached.

Blayze turned around. "Thanks for meeting me here. I've been looking over the side, and I can't see anything that could have caused so much damage from just a fall."

"Do you think she was pushed?" Ananda leaned over the balcony to have a look for himself.

"We need to do a sweep of all the open decks on this side to find out exactly where she went over from."

They started their search of each deck and, as they reached the front of Deck 5, they noticed a scuff mark on the railing. It was opposite a doorway, which would have been a simple escape for someone if they had thrown her over. Ananda leaned over where the scuff mark was but could see no sign of any marks on the deck below. "If she hit something, it wasn't around here," he said to Blayze, who was checking out the door.

"Where does this door lead?" Blayze asked.

"Just to the forward passenger elevators."

Blayze walked through, leaving Ananda outside. He looked around and saw no sign of a struggle. He headed back outside and closed the door. "Nothing through that way," he said, meeting Ananda, who was crouching down by the guttering at the edge of the deck.

"Is this a tooth?" questioned Ananda as he picked something out from near the drain.

"Let me have a look." Blayze took hold. "It certainly is. Question is, though, did it belong to Rachel? There's only one way to find out."

They took the tooth to the infirmary and asked to see the body again. The doctor pulled back the sheet once more.

"Doctor, can you hold her mouth open for me for a second? I want to check something out."

The doctor opened Rachel's jaw and Blayze held the tooth up close to see if it was hers.

"The colouring seems to match," he said, scanning the tooth along her remaining teeth. "Hang on." He placed the tooth into one of the gaps and it fit perfectly. "Without proper dental records we can't be one hundred per cent sure, but I would have to say that this here is Rachel's tooth, and now we have our murder site."

"I will put some tape around that area and block the exit to that door, making it look like it's having work done, so no one uses it," said Ananda, already taking out his phone to get the job done.

Blayze summarised their findings. "This means that some of her injuries were definitely sustained on board before she fell. But how?"

AS SIMON MADE HIS WAY down to meet the dancers, singers, musicians, and technical crew, he paused on the last step, his hand firmly gripping the railing next to him. He closed his eyes and uttered, "You can do this, be strong," to himself. After gathering his thoughts and taking a few deep breaths, he headed backstage where everyone had gathered. As soon as he got closer to them, the thought of what he was about to tell them overwhelmed him, which again stopped him in his tracks, frozen with nerves, anxiety and grief. A few people noticed him just standing there.

"Come on then, boss, what's so important you dragged us out of bed?" Andrew asked. Normally at that time, most of the dancers would be having their afternoon nap before show time.

Simon looked up and took another deep breath. For a split-second he wanted to turn away and run, but he knew that he couldn't, as his friends needed to hear this from him. He began walking the last few steps up the ramp, leading him onto the stage. Now standing in the middle, so everyone could see him, Simon paused and looked around. With no scenery out, and just the working lights on, the stage felt cavernous. The anticipation on their faces, not knowing what was about to come, was intense.

"Spit it out, then," Laura piped up.

"Hang on, where's Rachel?" asked Tammy, looking around.

More people started looking around in case they had missed her and she was hiding somewhere.

"Guys, guys, listen," Simon said, gaining people's attention. "I've got some terrible news and I need you to listen carefully to me." Everyone had stopped talking and their full focus was now on him. "Today, as you all know, we rescued someone who had gone overboard. Unfortunately, that person was Rachel." As soon as Rachel's name was mentioned, the looks on people's faces changed from anticipation to complete sadness.

"Is she okay?" asked Laura.

He hesitated and held his breath for a moment. With a tear rolling down his cheek, he let out a deep sigh. "It's with a heavy heart that I have to tell you all that Rachel unfortunately passed away not long after they got her to the medical centre." The tears began streaming down faces, people throwing their arms around each other in disbelief. Some people just sat in complete shock, not knowing how to react. "I know this is a shock to everyone, as it was to me, but we still don't know how, why, or what happened."

Laura stood up, walked over to him, and gave him a comforting hug. Simon was only just holding himself together, trying to be strong. As Laura pulled away, he grabbed her hand and held her close-by. "I want you all to know that I am here for each and everyone of you. I have agreed with Robert that tonight's show will be cancelled. Instead, the theatre will go dark in Rachel's memory. Her family has been informed, and Robert will make an announcement shortly to let everyone on board know there will be no show tonight."

"I can't believe it!" cried Francesca.

"Nor can I," Simon replied. "I know you will all have questions about what happened, and I promise you all, once I know more I will let you know." Simon thought it best not to tell them about what the doctor had said about the injuries to her face, as the news of her passing had taken its toll on people's emotions enough already. Some were sobbing uncontrollably. "For now, though, I think we need to remember Rachel for who she was. A funny, loving, amazing friend." Laura squeezed his hand tight and looked up at him. "We will miss you like mad," Simon said.

Simon couldn't speak anymore. His emotions poured out, and he broke down in front of everyone. Tears came streaming down his face as Laura hugged him again. While Laura embraced him, Simon turned them around so that his back was to everyone. He was embarrassed that he had shown such weakness at a time when they needed him most. Andrew noticed this and stood up and walked over to join in with the pair. It sparked everyone to get up and surround Simon, and it became a massive group hug, with tears flowing. The group stood there for a few minutes as no one wanted to let go. Eventually, Simon said, "Listen, guys, I need to see Robert to discuss everything." As the hug eased off, people parted to let Simon out.

"If you need to talk, call me," Andrew said to Simon as he passed, touching him on the shoulder to stop him.

Simon paused and looked into his tearful eyes. "Thanks, hun." He continued to exit and as he reached the door he glanced back, noticing the group hug had reformed, just this time, without him.

THE CAST, BAND AND technical crew remained backstage for some time. They talked about their memories of Rachel, and questions were asked about how something like that could have happened. It was almost teatime, yet many had lost their appetite and decided that they needed a drink instead. They filtered off, some heading straight for the crew bar, while others just wanted to be alone in their cabins. As people left, the lighting technician, Stuart, who had not been on the ship that long, came up with the idea of holding a memorial for Rachel later that night for anyone who wanted to come and pay their respects. The remaining few who were still there agreed it was a beautiful idea, as people could just turn up when they wished throughout the night.

"Does anyone have a photo that we could put in a frame?" Stuart asked.

"I've got a lovely one on my laptop," Andrew replied. "I'll ask one of the photographers to get it blown up for you and get it dropped off here ASAP, if that's okay?"

"That would be brill, thank you."

Everyone had now dispersed, leaving Stuart to set up. He had offered to do this as he didn't know Rachel as well as the others did, and knew that they needed to be with each other right now. At the back of the stage, he placed a stool for

Rachel's picture to sit on when it arrived. He headed to the lighting desk, which was out in the auditorium at the top of the circle. Knowing exactly which spotlight to put on, without even opening the curtains to see, the stool was fully lit. He dimmed all the other onstage lights and turned off the house lights completely. In the lighting booth, he found the 'No Entry' signs in a drawer under his desk. He placed them outside all the theatre doors on both floors before heading backstage. In one of the side storage rooms he knew he had seen some large battery-powered fake candles. They had been used for weddings in the past, he had been told, but he decided they would be perfect for the calm, peaceful setting he was trying to accomplish. He found them, replaced the old batteries with fresh ones, and set them around the stool. Once the picture of Rachel had arrived, he placed it on the stool and turned on all the candles.

"That's beautiful," a voice said, coming up the ramp to the stage.

Stuart turned around and noticed Andrew with a tear in his eye. "Glad you like it," he said, and was met with a hug.

"Let me buy you a drink," Andrew said, and lead Stuart to the crew bar.

CHAPTER SIX

Simon was back in his cabin and had just finished on the phone to his mum. He had needed someone to tell him everything would be okay, and he knew she would be the best one to call. There was a knock on the door, so Simon went to answer it, having locked it earlier for some privacy.

"Are you Simon?" said the man standing there, who Simon had never seen before.

"I am, sir, but I'm sorry, you can't be down here," he replied, as he had noticed the man wasn't wearing a crew name badge. Dressed in a Hawaiian shirt and shorts, Simon thought he looked like a typical passenger who had got lost. "How do you know...?" Simon began to ask, but the man interrupted.

"I was given your cabin information by Ananda, Chief of Security. Let me introduce myself. My name is Special Agent Blayze Carlson, FBI." Blayze held out his hand.

Simon's face went from 'just leave me alone' to 'holy shit' as his eyes widened. Having never been in any trouble with the law before, he became nervous having an FBI agent standing at his door. "How can I help you, sir?" Simon asked, slowly reaching his hand out to shake Blayze's.

"Can I come in for a moment?" Blayze asked.

"Erm, yeah, sure, come in." Moving out of the way, Simon let Blayze pass by him and gestured for him to sit on his desk chair. He closed the door and perched himself on the edge of his bed. Despite his anxiety at an FBI agent being in his room, he couldn't help but notice how gorgeous Blayze was, spotting his muscles popping out from under his shirt and his chiselled jawline, which had just a hint of stubble.

"Before I ask you anything, I just want to say how sorry I am to hear about your friend, Rachel."

"Thank you so much. It's all still a shock, really," Simon replied, shaking his head.

"I bet it is. Not something you could see coming, then? No signs of depression or anything like that?"

"No, not at all, sir." Simon was a little taken back at the implication that Rachel could have been depressed. "She was the life and soul of any room she walked into. The complete opposite, sir."

"Please, call me Blayze. 'Sir' is too formal, especially when I'm dressed like this. I'm meant to be on vacation, but Ananda has asked me to help as we've worked together before. I need to ask you a few questions, just to get to know more about Rachel, to piece everything together. Is that okay?"

"Yes, of course, ask away," Simon said, taking a deep breath. The tension in his shoulders eased as he became a little more relaxed knowing that he wasn't being interrogated.

"Was Rachel seeing anyone, do you know?"

"Well. She wasn't known for seeing anyone on a long-term basis, if you get what I mean. We found out just the other day, actually, that the captain had been a regular hook-up of hers."

"That's interesting, with him being missing, that is." Blayze tilted his head and looked upwards, trying to think if the two of them could have been involved in something. "Was there anyone else?" he continued.

"To be honest with you, there are probably dozens, but I couldn't tell you who. She had an argument with someone on the phone the other night, though, and as she saw me, she hung up and walked away. I was going to ask her about it today." Simon choked up, remembering the last time he had seen his friend. He looked to the ceiling and took another deep breath to stop him from crying. "But I never got the chance. Now we'll never know who she was talking to, will we?"

Blayze asked a few more questions about Rachel's lifestyle and personality. Once he had what he needed, he stood up and offered Simon his hand. "Thank you for your time. You've been very informative."

Simon reciprocated the handshake much more rapidly than he had done before. "Anything I can do to help, let me know."

"Much appreciated. Just one last thing. Her face was severely beaten. Can you think of anyone who would want to do that to her?"

"I've been asking myself the same question since the doctor told me about her injuries earlier. There's no one I know on here who would hurt a fly, let alone another human being."

"Thanks again, Simon. I'll see you at the meeting tonight." Blayze let himself out and closed the door behind him, not waiting for a reply.

Simon sat there for a while, wondering if he had missed out any information and wishing that he had just knocked on Rachel's door that night and asked her about the argument. Maybe none of this would have happened and she would still be alive if he had just stepped in earlier. Those thoughts, and the blame he was putting on himself, got Simon upset, and he lay on his bed, crying.

Another knock came at his door. Drying the tears from his eyes, Simon quickly got up and opened it.

"Here you go, mate, thought you might need one," said David, the musical director, holding two beers. He passed one over.

Simon took it, and before saying a word, took three large gulps. Wiping his lips, he stepped to one side. "Cheers, mate, I definitely needed that. Come in, come in." David walked in and sat himself down on the edge of the bed.

"I'm not going to stay long as I'm sure you've got loads to do and your dancers will need you. I just wanted to say I'm sorry to hear about Rachel. She was a lovely girl, and I'd known her for many years."

"Cheers, mate."

"I remember her first ever contract back in," he paused, trying to count the years in his head, "2004, I think it was. She was a spring chicken, fresh out of college and bloody stunning."

By this point, Simon had already finished his beer and opened his fridge, producing two more.

"Bloody hell, you're quick," David said as Simon handed him one. "Why not?" He shrugged his shoulders, took the beer that was being offered, and downed the one he had brought in with him. "To Rachel," he proposed, raising his newly given beer.

"To Rachel," Simon replied, and they both took a swig.

Not waiting to finish his beer, David started making his way to the door. "Listen, mate, I'll let you get back to it and catch up with you later."

"No worries, thanks for the drink. It's just what I needed," Simon said, sitting back down on the bed.

"Hey, before I go, who was that fella I saw leaving yours a few minutes ago? Are you two, you know..."

"Whoa, no, not at all," Simon jumped in. "That was the FBI."

David looked confused. "Dressed like that? How did they get here so quick?"

"He was already here."

"Ah, okay, cool. Anyway, mate, see you tonight." David headed out of the door.

"See you later," Simon got in just as the door shut. He sat there for a little while longer, finishing the beer he had just opened, but thought twice about having another one, especially with a full crew meeting happening later and now the FBI being there too. Still not feeling hungry, and with a couple of beers now inside him, Simon decided he had better take a brief nap in the hope he would feel better afterwards.

He lay back on his bed and closed his eyes, but all he could picture was Blayze stood at his doorway. The image of dragging him inside and throwing him down on the bed and then kissing his body all over was playing like a record on repeat in Simon's mind. "No, can't think like that," Simon told himself as he got off the bed. He headed to the bathroom and turned on the shower. Images like that were not going to help him sleep, so he freshened up before getting a coffee and some fresh air.

IT WAS NOW ELEVEN O'CLOCK and the main theatre was full with crew members from all departments. At the front of the stage, a row of chairs had been set up and in them, sitting waiting to start, Simon noticed, were the staff captain, chief security officer, the cruise director, and Blayze, who he had met earlier. They had pulled a curtain across behind them, covering Rachel's memorial from view. Andrew leaned closer into Simon and whispered in his ear.

"Who's that hunk on the stage?"

"You'll find out soon enough, don't you worry. Bit of a dish though, right?"

"You're telling me." Andrew put his hands together in prayer and looked up to the heavens. "One night, just give me one night."

"Well, he's already seen the inside of my cabin," Simon said, smirking at Andrew and giving him a cheeky wink. Just as Simon had replied, the staff captain stepped forward to address the awaiting crowd.

"You always have to have them first, don't you?" Andrew said, throwing his arms down, but before Simon could respond, Antonio began to speak, looking confident and calm.

"Thank you, everyone, for coming so late. We have called you here as we have some news that we must share with you all. Captain Argenti is not resting in his cabin, as people have been lead to believe. He is, in fact, missing, and has not been seen since Sunday evening." He paused for a second as gasps roared from the crowd in disbelief. "The coastguard have been informed and so have the police as this is now a missing persons case. We would, though, not like this news to reach the passengers, so it does not cause any panic. Also, before I hand you over to Robert, your cruise director, I would like to thank all those involved with today's man overboard rescue for your courage and bravery. That being said," he turned and looked at those sitting behind him, "Robert, can you come and say a few words, please."

Robert made his way to the front of the stage, looking at the cast members who were sitting on the seats directly in front of him. "Thank you, staff captain," he said as they shook hands. He stopped and faced the crew. "Ladies and gentlemen, like the staff captain has just said, thank you to all those who risked their own lives on that turbulent ocean today during the rescue. I made an announcement earlier regarding the reason we had cancelled this evening's performances and said that it was because of a technical fault. This was also not true. I didn't want anyone to find out before I had spoken to you all first. It is with deep sadness that I have to inform you all that the girl who was rescued earlier this afternoon, unfortunately, did not survive." Looking around, he saw the tears already rolling down his own department's faces.

"She was also one of our own," he continued. "Her name was Rachel Lawson, and she was a dancer and part of the entertainment team here on board. Our thoughts go out to all of Rachel's family and friends at this sad time and they have all now been notified. It is never easy to find out that one of your own has passed away, so if anyone would like someone to talk to, to help them get through this time of grief, please do not hesitate to get in contact with either myself, Simon, the dance captain, or your head of department, who have all offered to help. I know a lot of you knew Rachel and if you need some time off work, we will help you with that. Here to help us figure out what happened, I would like to introduce to you, Special Agent Blayze Carlson from the FBI." Robert stood aside as Blayze made his way forward. After shaking his hand, Robert returned to his seat.

"FBI," Andrew said as he leaned into Simon again. "Typical. That's a no-go, then."

"Thank you, Robert," Blayze began. "Good evening, everyone, and thank you all for being here. With a missing captain and now the death of one of your fellow crew members, I am here to assist with the ongoing investigation. I have met a few of you already as I have been on board as a passenger since Sunday. I will be going around the ship, asking people questions at various points, so please, don't worry, I'm just collecting as much information as I can at this time. If any of you here heard anything, or saw anything, regarding the disappearance of the captain or what may have happened to Rachel, please come forward and let us know straight away. I am here to help and will be working alongside the staff captain, the chief of security and the cruise director to understand what has happened. Thank you, all." Blayze walked back to his seat and Ananda made his way forward.

"Shame, as look at that arse," Andrew commented, watching Blayze walk back to his seat. Simon just shook his head.

"Hello, everyone. Due to not being able to come and see each of you individually, we have set up a mobile number for people to call if they noticed anything. Even if you think it may be nothing, please let us know by calling 0100 anytime, day or night. The phone line will be available twenty-four hours a day. We will stay around for a while now, in case anyone wants to come and speak to us in person. I have spoken to the staff captain, who has agreed that the planned general emergency drill that was to take place in Antigua, tomorrow, will now be postponed until next week. Thank you, everyone, for coming, and we want you to know that we are here for you all."

Having finished, Ananda made his way down the front steps onto the auditorium floor and was joined by Blayze, Robert and Antonio. They stood and talked among themselves as no one had approached them. Time passed and many of the crew members had left, with only a handful remaining, dotted around the theatre. Simon spotted Blayze, who had just finished talking to the staff captain and was heading his way. As he approached, Simon turned towards him.

"Don't worry, mate, we'll get to the bottom of all this, trust me," Blayze said, patting Simon's back.

"Thank you."

"Is everyone okay?"

"As best as they can be right now. It will take some time to sink in."

"It will, mate. It's never easy." He patted him again. Waving goodbye, Blayze headed out of the theatre.

Simon stood and watched everyone else leave until he was the last one remaining. He looked around the emptiness of the entire place, doing a 360-degree turn and noticing how eerily quiet it was. With a deep sigh, he turned his attention back to the stage and blew a kiss. "Goodnight, Rachel. We will miss you, sweetheart."

AFTER FINISHING AT the crew meeting, unable to sleep, Blayze had spent all night in his cabin, creating a collage on his walls of everything he knew about the captain and Rachel to see if there was a connection that no one knew about. It took some time, but it was his favourite thing to do as he could see people's lives right in front of him, and could normally spot things straight away. The problem he found, though, was that Rachel played around and was known by a vast amount of men, according to Simon and Robert. Blayze's list of potential suspects would cover all of his walls entirely once he knew all of their names, and it would make it difficult to narrow it down to just one person.

The coffee he had throughout the night, to keep him going, was wearing off and he was becoming tired. The pictures he was staring at had begun to merge into each other, so he decided it was time for some sleep. He picked up his watch that he had placed on the bedside table when he had arrived back at his cabin.

"Bloody hell." It was coming up to nine in the morning. He had been at this for almost nine hours and had come up with nothing. Just as he was undressing to get into bed, the morning announcement came over the tannoy system.

"Good morning, ladies and gentlemen, this is your cruise director, Robert, here with an update on our arrival into the port of St John on the beautiful island of Antigua. As I mentioned yesterday, we have done our very best to catch up on the time lost and will get there just a few hours after our original scheduled time. Because of this, we will be staying in Antigua two hours longer so that all booked tours can still go ahead as normal. We will arrive at approximately eleven-thirty and our new departure time will be six-thirty this evening. We hope you have an amazing day, and remember, don't forget that sunscreen."

Blayze had originally planned to get off and explore the island, as he had never been to Antigua before, but first he needed some sleep. He set his alarm for one o'clock so he could venture out in the afternoon. He closed the curtains, finished getting undressed and turned off all the lights before getting into bed.

He had only been asleep for a few minutes when his cabin phone rang. Turning the bedside lamp on, he got out of bed and picked up the phone. "Hello," he answered, displeased. It was Robert on the other end, letting him know that he had organised a gathering at Fort James beach for the whole of the entertainment department and he was welcome to tag along if he wanted to. As that was not what Blayze had in mind, he just thanked Robert and declined his offer. He wanted some time alone to try to at least see some sights that he had been encouraged to visit. Hanging up the phone, he went straight back to bed.

He had only just closed his eyes again when there was a knock at the door.

"Housekeeping."

Knowing how quick his room steward was, Blayze dived out of bed to answer the door before they opened it. Peeping his head around, trying to hide the fact he was naked, he quickly said, "I'm okay for now, thank you," and with a nod from his cabin steward he closed the door. Realising his mistake, he grabbed the 'do not disturb' sign and quickly opened the door and hung it on the handle.

'Right,' he thought, and made his way back to the bed, but before he could even sit down, his ship's mobile phone rang. Ananda had given him one so he could get hold of people from anywhere. "What?" he shouted, annoyed with all the disturbances.

"Is that Mr Carlson?" the voice on the other end said.

"Yes. How can I help you?" Blayze replied, calming down a little.

"My name is Andrew, and I'm one of the dancers."

"What can I do for you, Andrew?"

"Rachel and I were very close," he started.

"How close?" Blayze asked, knowing Rachel's history with men and needing to narrow down his search.

"She was like a sister to me, and totally the wrong gender, if that's what you're asking."

"So how can I help?"

"Well, I went round to Rachel's cabin last night to stay over with her room-mate and saw her laptop on the desk. I opened it up to see if she was still logged into anything. I thought I'd better ring you in case you wanted to have a look. Her Facebook, Twitter and emails are all open."

"Oh, yes please, that would be a massive help. Can you bring it up now? My cabin number is 6050."

"Yes, of course, I'll be there soon," Andrew replied.

Blayze hung up and threw the phone down on the bed. "Looks like I'm not getting any sleep." Not needing to get fully dressed, as he had no intention of letting anyone in, he slipped on some jogging pants. Jumping into the bathroom quickly, he brushed his teeth and sprayed plenty of deodorant on, remembering he'd been up all night. Blayze was looking forward to seeing how much information he could get from Rachel's social media sites, as nowadays everyone put their entire life online for the world to see. It was just what he was waiting for. The answers to all the questions he had could be on this one device.

It wasn't long before a knock came at the door and Blayze opened it, knowing full well who it would be. "Andrew, is it?" he asked.

"Yeah," Andrew replied, his eyes now scanning every inch of Blayze's body from head to toe. "Wow," he muttered and his jaw dropped.

Blayze coughed to bring Andrew's attention from his crotch to his face. "Is that Rachel's laptop?"

"Shit, sorry, yeah. Here you go." Andrew went to hand over the laptop but kept a grip of it, and as Blayze pulled it, Andrew moved in closer. He closed his eyes and breathed in. "You smell gorgeous."

"Erm, thanks," Blayze replied, shocked at how forward Andrew was. He pulled harder at the laptop, which soon left Andrew's hands. "I'll return it when I've finished with it." Blayze went to shut the door and Andrew stepped back.

"Is there anything else I can do for you?" Andrew asked, trying to get his last view of Blayze's chiselled abs.

"All good for now. Thanks for this." Noticing Andrew's eyes all over him, he reached down and scratched his balls, moving his penis, knowing Andrew's focus would be straight down there. "I'll leave you with that," he said and closed the door. Looking through the peephole, he noticed Andrew hadn't moved and was just standing there in a daze, mouth open.

He walked over to the desk and put down the laptop. "They are so easy to tease," he said, shaking his head. It wasn't the first time he had been hit on by a gay guy, and he knew it wouldn't be the last. He opened up the laptop to see what she had left open. "Now then, Rachel, what have you been hiding?"

CHAPTER SEVEN

Having finally arrived in Antigua, Simon stood on the pier and waited for the rest of the dancers to debark. It was almost half past twelve and the sun was beaming down, already burning his skin. Simon would hardly ever sit and sunbathe for more than fifteen minutes at a time. He loved the sun, but had been burnt that many times before he'd had enough blisters to last him a lifetime. He had his Factor 50 on his face, legs and arms while keeping on a navy blue T-shirt, knee-length shorts, and trainers. One by one the cast joined him, enveloping him like a sea of skin, all of them dressed in the skimpiest of outfits. The rest of the entertainment team soon joined and, once Robert had arrived, they set off walking to the taxi rank. They had to wait a while as the crowds of passengers were also there, queueing with them. It was also the pickup site for many of the tours that people had booked, further extending their wait.

"I've planned something special for when we get there," Robert said to the crowd, though some of them missed the announcement as they were far too deep in their own conversations.

"As long as there are some hammocks free in the shade, I'm good," Simon replied, to which Robert, noticing what Simon was wearing, just rolled his eyes.

Simon went and stood under a tree to get out of the sun as it was glaring down on them, making him sweat already.

He could hear people asking Robert about the surprise, but he wasn't giving anything away and told them they would need to wait and see. After finishing his second cigarette, Simon noticed that all the department had finally reached the front of the queue and he went over to join them, standing next to Robert and David.

"Right, come on, you lot. Get in," Robert ordered as their first ten-seater taxi pulled up. "Tell the driver you want to go to Fort James Beach and that I'll sort out payment when we all get there." Once Simon and David were in, he closed the taxi door, leaving the rest of them stood waiting. As they pulled away, Simon noticed two more taxis arriving just behind them, so soon enough, everyone would be on their way to the beach.

It was only a six-minute drive to Fort James by taxi and, once everyone had arrived, Robert gathered them all together. They could see the beach through the trees in front of them, and the bright blue water glistened in the sunlight, tempting them to run straight to it.

"I know not all of you want to stay at the beach all day, but I just wanted to get us all together as a team," Robert explained. "We've been through a lot these past couple of days and we need to stick together. Everything for the next few hours is on me."

"Get in!" Andrew piped up, rubbing his hands together.

Simon saw Robert throw Andrew a look, one that suggested he would be keeping an eye on him, silencing him quickly and making him instantly drop his hands. "I've already booked us tables at this restaurant," Robert continued, pointing to a building just a few hundred yards from where they were all standing, "then afterwards there is an open tab on the beach bar for an hour; just say my name. Let's get some food." And with that, he led the group towards the restaurant.

"Did you know he was going to do this?" David asked Simon, having crept up behind him.

Simon jumped. "Jesus, don't scare me like that!" he shouted. "No, I didn't. He just told me to make sure everyone was ready on the pier by twelve-thirty."

"Nice of him to get this organised for us all. It's not every day we can all get together like this."

"Very true. Now let's get in, I'm bloody starving." Simon patted David on the back and they walked inside, eager to eat some local cuisine.

THEY SPREAD OUT ACROSS several tables, all ready for something to eat. The smell of the fried onions and garlic, along with fish and beef, that was coming from the kitchen was incredible and they couldn't wait to try it all. Robert had organised a tapas-style lunch, and the restaurant staff kept bringing more and more dishes to every table. Food and drink flowed for just over an hour until Robert could see people ready to leave, so he went to settle the bill. At the counter, he turned around to look at everyone, noticing how some were in deep conversation, and others were erupting with laughter. 'At least they are all okay and happy,' he thought. He looked down at the bill that the barman had placed in front of him.

"Bloody hell, you lot! How to bankrupt someone in under two hours," he jested towards the crowd behind him as he pulled out his wallet, flashing the many hundred-dollar bills he had brought with him.

Once the bill was settled, he made his way back to the table at which he had been sitting. "Whenever you want to, guys, just make your way to the beach." Within seconds, people had gathered their belongings and made their way outside. The beach was right on the restaurant's doorstep, so they didn't have far to go. Simon headed straight for the nearest hammock under the nearby trees, and many of the department went towards the water's edge, laying down their beach towels and applying yet more sunscreen. Robert and David, however, had set their sights on the bar, which was close to Simon in his hammock.

"You want a beer bringing over?" Robert asked Simon.

"Oh, go on then, why not."

He turned back to David and leaned on the bar. "What are you having?"

"Rum and coke, please."

Robert ordered the round of drinks, and once they had arrived, he handed Simon his beer. "There you go, mate. Take some time for yourself, today, and recharge. It's not easy being in charge, and the one that people turn to when there is a problem, but you've been amazing for all of them." They both looked out to see the dancers having fun in the ocean and enjoying themselves trying to dive off each other's shoulders.

"Thank you, and yeah, I will. I appreciate all your support." They raised their drinks for a silent 'Cheers', then Robert headed back to the bar.

FOR THE NEXT HOUR, rounds of drinks were ordered, and people enjoyed the sun and the sea. Simon relished the peace and quiet and loved the relaxing sound of the waves rolling on the shore. Being in the shade was enough for him as he was still sweating from just the heat of the day. He looked over at his dancers and noticed Andrew and Laura packing up their things. Before they left, they headed straight to Simon. "Where are you two off to?" he asked.

"We'd already booked an afternoon boat ride to see the Pillars of Hercules. My mum saw them when she cruised ages ago and she said they are amazing," Laura replied.

"Alright, you guys, have fun. I'll see you back on board later."

"Thanks for today, boss," Andrew said.

"Don't thank me, this was all Robert's idea. And his money."

"Thanks, Robert!" Andrew turned and shouted as loud as he could.

"What are you like?" Simon responded, knowing what was about to happen. As expected, Andrew's outcry started a wave of thank yous from various sections of the beach. Andrew looked back at Simon and just winked, before he and Laura started walking away.

Making use of everyone shouting 'thank you', Robert stood up and waved. "Tab's now closed, you're on your own." He sat back down to finish his drink and paid the bartender what he owed.

Simon got out of his hammock and walked towards the bar. "Thanks for today, they've needed this," he said, shaking Robert's hand. "I'm gonna head back, though, and get a nap. The heat really takes it out of me."

"I'll come back with you," Robert replied. "I've got loads to do to make sure the rest of the cruise goes to plan."

"I'm gonna stay for a little while longer," David added, still sitting at the bar, while Robert stood up and thanked the barman. "Same again, please," David ordered.

"Catch you later," Robert said, and left with Simon, who had waved goodbye to anyone who was looking.

As the two friends got into a taxi, Robert sat back in his seat and patted Simon's leg. "No shows and no duties for you guys tonight, so just relax and enjoy your time off."

"I plan to, but if you need me, just call. Today's been just what I needed."

"My pleasure."

They sat and peered out of the window, watching the world pass by while heading back to the ship. Simon pondered what to do with his evening. He wanted to see Blayze, to see if he'd had any luck finding out any answers, but apart from that, perhaps an early night was in order.

BLAYZE HAD SPENT A few hours going through Rachel's laptop and had written a lot down already. He planned to get out and off the ship for a few hours, though, not wanting to miss the reason he was on the cruise in the first place. After getting himself ready, he headed to the gangway, wondering what to do with the little time he had left. He decided to just go for a brief walk wherever the mood took him, as he had not slept since the day before and was too tired to venture far. He ended up in Victoria Park and, instead of walking further, decided to have a lie down on the grass to soak up a bit of sun.

Although it should have been a time of relaxation, his mind was still racing with what he had seen on Rachel's laptop. Having already seen photos of the many guys she was friends with or had slept with, he wondered if any of them were on board and, if so, why they would attack her in such a brutal way.

It was mid-afternoon, and the sun wasn't as strong as it had been, but it was still shining brightly enough to top up his tan. The trees glistened and cast shadows on the grass beside him, but unfortunately he wasn't that far away from the city, so the sound of traffic nearby meant that it wasn't as relaxing as had hoped. He took off his short-sleeved shirt and vest and placed them on the ground. Lying back, he closed his eyes and put his hands behind his head. He could feel the warmth all over his body as the sun shone on his face and shaved torso. As he lay there, he tried to push the investigation out of his mind so that he could relax for a time and enjoy a part of his vacation. He hadn't had much time out in the sun, and this was his chance.

"Taking some time off?" a voice said above him. As he opened his eyes, he saw the two girls from the gym who had been staring at him during his workout.

Blayze sat up and put one hand over his eyes to block the sun so he could see them properly. He noticed them staring at his body yet again. "Yeah. What are you guys up to?"

"We've just been to the beach with everyone and fancied a little walk before heading back. I'm Alice, by the way, the assistant cruise director on board, and this is Tammy, one of the dancers."

"Nice to meet you both. Listen, sorry about your friend."

"Thanks, but she wasn't really a friend," Tammy said, folding her arms. "We fell out a few years back when she stole my boyfriend from underneath me."

"Really? Who was that?" Blayze probed.

"Oh, he's not around anymore. He went to work for a different cruise line soon after he found out she was also hooking up with his cabin-mate."

"You never told me that part," Alice jumped in.

"So she got around, then," Blayze added.

"Just a bit, yeah. Still, I wouldn't have wished this on her. I may have wished her harm a few times in the past, but this was a shock. Do you know who did it yet?" Tammy asked.

"Not yet. We are still compiling evidence and I've now got her laptop, but it will take me a while to find out who everyone is in the pictures."

"There are plenty of exes on board, which will keep you busy," Tammy remarked.

"Really?" Blayze replied. That was what Blayze had considered earlier, and now that he had his answer, he needed names.

"Yes," Alice replied. "If you need our help, we would gladly assist you," she said while linking arms with Tammy.

"Yeah, we would gladly help you," Tammy added, grinning at Alice.

Noticing the little smirk from Tammy, Blayze knew that all they really wanted was to spend more time with him. "That's great. If you could pop by my cabin later, 6050, with a list of exes you know, that would be helpful. I'll see you back on board in a bit. Need to catch a few more rays, first." The girls walked away and Blayze lay back down with his hands behind his head. He closed his eyes but could still hear little giggles coming from his admirers.

The sound of the girls' voices had only just disappeared into the distance when a loud scream suddenly came from the direction in which they had walked. Blayze darted up and ran that way, leaving his vest and shirt on the ground. He headed straight for the trees but was faced with a choice of three paths. Not knowing which path the girls had taken, he plumped for the middle one and continued to run when he heard another scream from his left. Changing direction, he jumped over some fallen logs, ducking and diving through the branches hanging down, until he came across a female lying face down in the twigs and leaves just ahead of him.

He recognised the clothing; it was Alice. He ran up to her and rolled her body over. He knelt down, placing two fingers on her wrist to check for a pulse, and placed his ear to her mouth to check for any sign of breath.

There was neither.

"Shit," he muttered to himself. He looked around, but there was no sign of Tammy. The sound of a twig snapping gripped his attention, and he stood back up and ran in the direction it had come from. In the distance, he spotted someone running away through the trees and followed, sprinting as fast as he could through the overgrowth under his feet, when his foot got caught on something, causing him to trip and fall over.

As he stood up, ready to continue the chase, he looked at what he had tripped over. It was Tammy. There was a rustle on the ground as Tammy moved her fingers. He knelt down by her head to check her pulse, but it was weak. He glanced back up, but the person he was chasing had disappeared. Returning his focus to Tammy, he noticed blood pouring from underneath her. When he looked closer, he saw that someone had stabbed her multiple times in the side and chest.

"Help!" he screamed. "Somebody help me!" But it was too late. Tammy took her last breath and died in his arms.

After placing Tammy's lifeless body back on the ground, with his hands and body now covered in blood, he reached into his pocket and called his boss at the FBI. "I need you to get the local police to my location now. I have two dead bodies and a potential serial killer on board the ship. The two murders are too closely related to be random."

"Okay, they are on their way," his boss replied. "The cruise will have to be cut short and you have to tell them that they need to head straight back to Miami. Now."

"Agreed."

"No one is to be allowed to leave the ship until the killer has been caught."

"I'm on it, boss."

Blayze waited in position until the local police arrived with ambulances to take the girls away. After going back to collect his vest and shirt, a police officer gave him a lift back to the cruise ship as well as a towel to clean the blood from his hands and body, though Tammy's blood still remained all over his shorts.

As he arrived at the pier, he noticed the long line of people queueing to get back on board, laughing, joking and still finishing off their drinks. The atmosphere was completely at odds with what he had just experienced. He waited patiently to make sure he was the last on the ship, so that no passengers or crew saw him. As he noticed the last people boarding, he made his way to the gangplank.

"Blayze, what's happened? Are you okay?" Ananda asked, looking directly at the amount of blood on Blayze's shorts.

Blayze quickly pulled Ananda over to one side so that no one else could hear him. "I've got some dreadful news. Two more people are dead."

"Don't tell me, it's Alice, the assistant cruise director, and Tammy, one of the dancers."

"Yeah, how did you know?" he asked, confused as he had not long left them and was yet to tell anyone on board.

"They are the only two people who have not returned. Simon and Robert are actually on their way down here now to see if they are running late."

"I'll wait here for them, then, as they need to know what's happened."

Blayze didn't have to wait long as the elevator across the way opened and Robert emerged on his phone. Simon had also just come around the corner on his phone, and they both walked towards the gangway that had been pulled up.

"Here they are now," Ananda said, pointing Blayze to their direction.

"What's going on?" Robert said, putting his phone back in his pocket. "I can't get hold of Alice or Tammy."

"I've asked a few people," Simon replied, "and they said they went for a walk once the taxi dropped them all off."

"Guys, I've got some dreadful news," Blayze started, but the blood on his shorts had not gone unnoticed by either of them.

"No, not Alice and Tammy!" Robert shook his head in disbelief.

"I'm afraid so. I tried to chase the perpetrator, but they got away. Tammy was still alive and I couldn't leave her there. Unfortunately, she died in my arms moments later."

Simon burst into tears and put both hands over his face. "What is going on?" he sobbed.

"We need a meeting with Antonio now as we have to head back to Miami before anyone else gets hurt. If my suspicions are correct and these murders are all linked, then our murderer is on board right now."

"I'll make the call now," Ananda said in haste as his crew packed up the rest of the equipment ready to set sail.

"Thank you," Blayze replied. "Let me get changed and I'll meet you up there. Head straight to Antonio's office and don't tell anyone anything yet. We need to be careful."

All four of them got into the crew elevator. Blayze could see the look of sadness and shock all over Robert and Simon's faces with the news he had just delivered. He got out early and rushed to his cabin to throw on some clean clothes, while the other three made their way to Antonio's office.

CHAPTER EIGHT

Antonio, Simon, Robert and Ananda were sitting, waiting for Blayze to arrive. Robert had given Antonio as much information as he could and Simon sat in silence, still in shock at hearing dreadful news, yet again. There was a knock on the door, and without waiting for a response, Blayze entered.

"What happened, exactly?" Antonio asked.

Blayze started at the beginning, from when the girls had run into him at Victoria Park. He told them all, word for word, what they had said and how he had chased someone away.

"When the police came, I was able to have another look at the bodies. Alice had been hit on the back of the head with a sharp instrument, and upon closer inspection we noticed someone had snapped her neck, killing her instantly."

"Oh, dear God!" cried Robert. "Who could do such a thing?"

"Looking at Tammy's body, she had been stabbed twice in the chest and three times in the side, as if she had been held from behind by her attacker. Unfortunately, she suffered the longest, as her attacker must have heard me coming and didn't finish the job."

"What the hell do we do and say to everyone?" questioned Antonio, shocked by the vivid description of their brutal murders.

"As of right now, we are the only ones who know what happened, plus their killer, of course," Blayze started as he began pacing the room. "We don't know yet if their murders are linked to Rachel's and the disappearance of the captain. Only the killer knows that. We need to play this carefully and hope the killer slips up by asking questions only they would know. For now, let's tell everyone that they were just late and missed the ship."

"Good idea," Ananda added in. "Ship's protocol is that they would have to make their own way to the next port."

"Here lies the other problem," Blayze said, still pacing around.

"Can you please just sit down?" Simon said, staring directly at Blayze. He pushed his chair back and stood up. "Here, take mine."

"Is everything okay?" asked Blayze, walking towards Simon.

"All this news about more of my friends being murdered, and then you pacing behind me, I can't cope."

Blayze opened his arms and gave Simon a hug. "Listen. Everything will be okay, we just need to stick to a plan and try to keep everyone safe." He patted him on the back twice and then released him. "You good?" Blayze waited until Simon looked him directly in the eyes. "Hey."

"Yeah, I'm good." The sadness in his tone made Blayze give him another hug.

Blayze took a seat while Simon leaned against the wall near the door. All eyes were now on Blayze to see what further news he had.

"I spoke with my bosses and they have instructed that the cruise ends here and we sail back to Miami immediately."

"The passengers are going to love that news," Robert immediately slipped in.

"I know, but it's safer not to let anyone else off the boat as we now have the killer trapped on here."

"Safer? Really?" Simon asked. "What about the rest of us?"

"If we have to lie and say something like Norovirus has spread, we could keep everyone in their own cabins for a period of time. We need to keep that as a last resort, though, when we know we have our killer."

Antonio rubbed his chin, deep in thought, and sat upright. "We will wait until tomorrow morning to announce the diversion back to Miami. We will say we have a problem with our engines and need to head back at a steady pace."

"Excellent idea," Blayze jumped in.

"I will let the cast know that Tammy missed the ship and will join us at the next port," Simon declared.

"Thank you, Simon," Robert said, looking back at him. "I will let the rest of the team know that Alice also missed the ship and will catch up with us soon."

"Keep an eye out for any signs. The killer will know you are lying and may ask questions to see if you know more," Blayze said, glancing at them both. "That goes for anyone you mention it to," he added, bringing his attention back to the rest of the room. "If there is anyone who you think knows more, I need to know right away."

"Secure this ship as best you can and add in some extra patrols," Antonio said, focussing directly at Ananda. "I want this murderer found."

"Yes, sir," Ananda replied with a nod of his head.

Antonio arose from behind his desk and walked towards the door. "Thank you, everyone. Let's meet here tomorrow morning at 08:30 to discuss what we will say to the passengers and crew, and also for an update on finding this killer." He opened the door, and Blayze and Robert stood and followed Simon out of the office.

"Tell only who you need to tell, and I'll be in my cabin if you need me," Blayze said to Simon and Robert. "I've still got a lot of things to look through on Rachel's laptop. Catch you guys later and remember, be careful."

They all went their separate ways, each with a job to do.

AFTER MAKING A FEW phone calls to pass the word around that Tammy and Alice had missed the ship, Simon headed to the bow of the ship to have a smoke in the crew area. As he arrived, he could hear the band playing on the Lido deck for the sail away party, all going as planned. He noticed Andrew sitting by himself on a sun lounger soaking up even more rays, as if he hadn't had enough already at the beach earlier. Simon wished he could have a body as tanned as Andrew's, but he and the sun just didn't go together, and instead of going brown, he just ended up like a lobster.

Lying over the phone about the girls missing the ship was one thing, but telling someone face-to-face was Simon's biggest worry. He paused for a brief moment. Taking in a long, deep breath, he mustered the courage to face his problem head on. "You can do this," he said, giving his body a little shake.

"Hey there," he said while walking over to where Andrew was lying. "You've probably not heard, yet."

"What's wrong?" Andrew replied, lowering his sunglasses slightly to peer over the top of them.

"Tammy and Alice missed the ship."

"Any fucking need. Those two, when they get together, have no clue at all."

"I know, right?" Simon said with a nervous laugh. He sat down next to him and lit a cigarette. "Want one?" he asked, offering his pack along with his lighter.

"Go on, then, since you're offering." He took one and passed the packet back.

"And the lighter," Simon encouraged, noticing Andrew had gone to place it in the pocket of his shorts.

"Shit, sorry. Force of habit." He passed the lighter over and lay down, pushing his glasses back on properly. "So are they gonna meet us tomorrow?"

"That's the plan, yeah. Where did they go to, anyway?" he questioned, to see if Andrew knew anything about their plans.

"Who knows? We all got a taxi back together, and they walked off in the opposite direction to us. Laura and I came straight back here."

"Oh well, we will see them tomorrow." Simon paused and took a drag of his cigarette while thinking of what to say next. "Good job we ain't got a show, isn't it?" he said, trying to change the conversation.

"True that. You gonna be back up later for a drink?" Andrew asked, noticing Simon had nearly finished his cigarette.

"Maybe. Give me a ring later on if you're up here and if it's not too busy, I'll join you." Simon stood up and docked his cigarette out in the ashtray on the nearby table. "See you in a bit," he said as he walked away. Andrew just threw his arm up to gesture a wave goodbye but said nothing.

As soon as Simon got to the door, he breathed a sigh of relief. "That wasn't too bad," he muttered.

Wanting a distraction, Simon headed up to the Lido deck to see how the party was going. As he got up there, he noticed a full dancefloor, everyone joining in with the Cha Cha Slide. As he walked closer, the music had got to the 'Everybody clap your hands' section, and he joined in while continuing to walk past, encouraging those sitting at the tables, near the all-you-can-eat buffet, to join in too. Some did, but most were too busy stuffing their faces with burgers and fries — a regular sight every time he walked across that deck. People would finish their lunch or dinner and still head up to queue for more to eat on the Lido deck. Every cruise there was so much wasted, but the passengers just saw it as 'free food! Why not?'.

As he continued walking, passing the pool at the centre of the deck, a female passenger stopped him. He recognised her from when Rachel had been in the water. She was the one who wouldn't move and here she was again, stopping Simon from walking any further, with yet another cocktail in her hand.

"Hey there..." she said, staring at his name tag. "...Simon."

"Hi," he replied, aiming not to get into a lengthy conversation.

"Listen, I'm sorry for getting in the way the other day. My husband told me off afterwards and I've been trying to look for you to apologise."

"Please don't worry. I need to..."

"It's just, I'd had a lot to drink already. You know, these cocktails are great!" she said, shoving the drink she had into Simon's face. "But they are lethal after having three or four."

"What number's this one?" Simon asked, pushing the drink away from his face.

"Numero dos," she replied, holding two fingers in the air. "Oh my God, you're a dancer!" she said after taking another looking at his name tag. "Show me some moves, then." She stepped back to give him some room, as if he was a performing monkey.

"I'll save them for the show, thanks." Noticing the space she had now produced by stepping aside, Simon saw his opportunity and scooted past her. "Gotta dash, need to practise some new steps for you," he said and hurried away.

"See you on the stage!" she shouted after him, waving her cocktail in the air.

After getting away, he didn't want another run-in with anyone. There were too many drunk people already and it wasn't even eight in the evening yet. Seeing all the food on people's tables had reminded him he hadn't eaten since the lunch on the beach, but with everything that had gone on, he couldn't really stomach a full meal. He knew that in his cabin he still had a few snacks left that he had bought in Miami, so thought it best to hide away for a while to get some peace and quiet. As he went through the doorway to make his way down the stairs, he noticed Robert coming up them.

"You okay, mate?" Robert asked as he reached the top step.

"Yeah, I'm just going down to mine for some time alone. You?"

"Here if you need me, okay?" Robert said as he walked past him. "Just want to make sure sail away is going as planned."

"I doubt they've even realised we're back at sea, as most of them are that drunk already. Anyway, see you later." Simon waved and proceeded downstairs with his head held low, not wanting to catch eyes with anyone.

BLAYZE HAD RUSHED BACK to his cabin and quickly tried to rinse as much blood off his clothes as he could. He had just thrown them onto the bathroom floor while getting changed earlier, and the blood had now dried and soaked in. After ten minutes of scrubbing them, he hung them in the shower so they could dry off, and went straight to his desk, where he had left Rachel's computer.

Opening the laptop, the screen lit up with the photos section of Rachel's Facebook page, which he had already started analysing. He had only gone back one year and already had a list of forty men's names written on his notepad. Before getting off the ship earlier, he had emailed Ananda for a manifest of all the passengers and crew so he could cross-reference any names with those who may be on board. Scrolling through more photos and writing even more names, he realised this would take hours. He then thought the easiest thing to do would be to start with the crew, and to search for their names in her friends list and on her profile. If there wasn't a match, he could cross them out. With over 1500 crew members to go through, seventy-five per cent being male, it was going to take him all night.

To keep himself going, he phoned room service and ordered his favourite Monte Cristo sandwich and some coffee.

After several hours of searching, Blayze had narrowed the list and a pattern had begun to emerge. He had seen that Rachel, although it seemed like she slept with everyone, preferred men who were older than her. That gave Blayze the opportunity to cross out anyone younger than twenty-five, giving a couple of years leeway in case she ever broke her pattern and fancied a change. The list of the crew was now down to 387, and names were easier to cross off when he couldn't find them on her profile. It would have been a much quicker process if Alice and Tammy had still been alive, he thought, as they had offered to give him all of their information. He kept going until the number of crew reached forty-five, and all of those names were people that Rachel had had some kind of relationship with in the past. 'Imagine having forty-five exes in one place,' he thought to himself.

Then it was time for the passengers. There were over 3500 names to go through on that list, but he used the same method as before. Females gone, under twenty-fives gone, and he also took off the over-sixties, knowing that was older than Rachel's father, and in her photos he hadn't seen her with anyone near that age apart from him. After a long, gruelling search, not one name matched. "So it's a crew member," he said out loud, picking up the list of names.

After taking down everything he had already stuck on his walls, he put all forty-five names up around the room, each on a separate piece of paper, giving them their own profile. He would now have to go through each name one by one and write as much information as he could find. He needed to know when their relationship was, how long it lasted, how it ended, whether anyone else was involved, if the guy was in a current relationship, and if there was a link between him and Alice and Tammy. One way to get some of that information would be to ask him directly, but that may give away that he was after him.

Yet there was one person he could ask: Robert. His name was on the list, too. He called and asked Robert to come to his cabin as soon as he could. While he was waiting, he started on some other names. The captain's name was on the list but he could put a line through him already as, with him not being found, and given the time frame since his disappearance, Blayze had already come to the conclusion that he was probably dead. A knock came at the door and Blayze went to answer.

"You asked for me," Robert said, walking straight in. He then noticed all the names on pieces of paper around Blayze's cabin. "Wow, you've been busy."

"I need to ask you a few questions regarding Rachel." Blayze pulled out his chair for Robert to sit on, then sat on the edge of his bed.

As Robert went to sit down, Blayze clocked him staring up at his name on a sheet on the wall.

"Okay, go ahead," Robert said, then pointed at the wall. "Can I just ask..."

"Well, this is why you're here. I've put together all the people Rachel had some sort of relationship with and there are forty-four names who all are on this cruise right now, not including the captain."

"Forty-four exes on the same ship? Bloody hell," Robert remarked.

"I'm trying to find out when these relationships were and how they ended. When were you two involved?"

"My God, it was years ago, now. Six or seven, maybe, and it lasted about two months. It was at the end of one of her contracts when I was still a host." Robert sat back in his chair, looking sad, as he recalled their time together. "We hooked up, and it became a regular thing. We knew we would both be heading our separate ways when the contract finished, so it ended mutually. We've worked together since then in the past, but never got together again as I was in another relationship by that time."

"And what about now?" asked Blayze, writing all of the recent information down and circling when their relationship was and how it ended.

"Single, at the moment. I got married to that girl I just mentioned, but she ran off with the staff captain a year later. I've not wanted any relationships recently, as this was only six months ago."

"Sorry to hear about that."

"Don't worry about it. Taught me a big lesson about relationships on ships. Don't bloody have one." They both chuckled at his remark.

Robert looked around at some of the names and was able to give Blayze bits of the information he needed. As Rachel was not shy about her love life, Robert knew when, where and how about quite a few of the men. He sat there with Blayze for almost two hours, filling in paper after paper with him until he knew no more.

After thanking him for helping, Blayze showed Robert the door and continued the paperwork by himself for another hour, using Rachel's laptop to search for any clues. Wanting to get a good night's sleep after not getting any the night before, he shut the laptop and turned the lights off. As much as he hated leaving things unfinished, his questions would have to wait until tomorrow.

EIGHT-THIRTY HAD COME and gone, and Robert was in his cabin, ready to announce to the passengers and crew that they would not be visiting St Lucia. After the morning meeting with Antonio, he had come up with a full events schedule so that there would be activities happening throughout the day to soften the blow. They had already made phone calls to the hotel director and chief purser, warning them that there would be some unhappy customers, and to the shore excursion desk to refund any tours that had been booked, so he could mention that in his speech. They had agreed that the excuse would be engine problems, and that to reach Miami on time they would have to sail at a steady speed and not stop.

With a little tap on the door, which Robert had left ajar, David popped his head into Robert's cabin. "Morning, Robert, can I come in?" Despite asking, he had already walked in, so Robert couldn't say no.

"Morning, David. How are you?"

"Yeah, man, all good."

"Have you wet the bed or something? Not like you to be up this early," Robert said, noticing how cheerful David looked for that time of the morning.

"Just waiting to get off. I love this port."

"Got some unpleasant news, sorry. Just sit there for a moment; I need to make a quick announcement."

David sat and listened while Robert told everyone that they would not be docking at St Lucia and that they had plenty of things planned for them.

"Sorry about that, how can I help you?" Robert asked, turning back round in his chair to face David, who was sitting on the couch near the window, now with a puzzled look on his face.

"Engine problems? Seriously?"

"That's what I've been told this morning by Antonio. I'm just the messenger."

"I don't believe that for one minute. Something else is up."

Robert sat back in his chair, attempting to look relaxed and desperately trying not to give away too much information. He had known David for many years, though, and asked himself what harm it could do. An extra pair of eyes, surely. He already knew about Rachel and the missing captain.

"Keep this to yourself, promise me." Robert leaned forward in his chair, awaiting David's response.

"Promise. What is it?" Eager to hear what Robert was about to say, David slid himself along the sofa closer to Robert so he didn't have to speak any louder than necessary.

"Alice and Tammy didn't just miss the ship. There was an incident in Antigua, in some park. Blayze was nearby and chased the attacker but didn't get them as Tammy was still breathing when he found her."

David sat back. "Is she okay? What about Alice?"

"Unfortunately, neither of them made it." Robert looked closely to see what David's reaction to the news was, but there was no expression at all. He had just stopped moving and was staring into space. "We don't know who the killer is but Blayze is working on that now. He may want to speak to you later, anyway."

Coming out of his little daydream, David shook his head to wake himself back up. "What? Why would he want to see me?" he snapped, sounding panicked.

"You dated Rachel at one point and he is trying to put the pieces together." Robert noticed beads of sweat now appearing on David's forehead. "Something wrong, mate? You're sweating there."

Wiping his forehead with his sleeve, he shook his head. "Just warm in here, that's all. Well, if we ain't docking today then I may as well go back to bed for a little while." David stood up and walked around the table, despite that route being longer than just walking past Robert.

"Okay, mate, see you later." He watched as David left.

Leaning back in his chair, he first questioned if his cabin was hot. Maybe it was a little, but it wasn't making him sweat. Then he questioned the vacant expression on David's face when he had told him about the girls. Was he not letting up on something? Realising that he had now told someone, Robert picked up the phone and called Simon.

"Hey, man, sorry to bother you. Can you come to my cabin shortly? Something's bothering me and I need to tell you about it."

Simon's response meant that he would be there in fifteen minutes, which gave Robert just enough time to grab a quick coffee. He grabbed a highlighter and was marking off all of the planned activities when he heard his door open again, but this time there was no voice. "Come in," he shouted, being used to people just popping in all the time. He continued checking out what else he could potentially put on for the extra sea day, then he realised no one had entered the room. He hadn't heard the door close.

"Anyone there?" he asked as he stood up and walked around the corner to see who had come in. Just as he turned, he was met with a blow to the face which knocked him straight to the floor.

CHAPTER NINE

Blayze had been up since six o'clock, sifting through Rachel's laptop. He had noted down another five relationships that had lasted longer than three months with men that were currently on board, before attending the morning meeting that had been planned. During the meeting, Blayze had explained his findings and that he was going to talk to each of the men to discuss their relationship with Rachel. It had been agreed that the excuse for missing St Lucia was to be engine problems and that they must head back to Miami straight away.

He was now back in his cabin awaiting a potential witness who had called the hotline while he had been on his way back from the meeting. Her name was Maruska, and she worked in the casino. So far, that's all he knew.

He continued to scroll through pictures of Rachel and came across one from 2015, which included David. Researching further, he noticed that their relationship had lasted for six months, but Facebook showed nothing about how or why they had broken up. Making a note of what he had found on David's sheet, he tried calling his cabin in order to attempt to fill in some gaps. The phone rang and rang, but there was no answer.

A knock came at the door, so Blayze hung up his call and answered it. A girl in her mid-twenties was standing with her feet together, arms in front of her body, holding onto a small black clutch bag. "You must be Maruska, right?"

"Da," she replied.

"Come in, come in," he ushered, letting Maruska in and closing the door behind her. He gestured to the chair he had just been sitting on. "Please sit."

She obliged and sat down, crossing her legs and placing her bag on her lap continuing to hold it with a tight grip.

"Please don't be nervous," Blayze said, noticing her staring at the floor. "I'm glad you came forward. Every bit of information is vital." He sat on his bed and grabbed his notepad and pen. "I can tell by your uniform that you work in the casino, correct?"

"Da," she replied again.

"Russian, I'm guessing?"

"Da, I mean yes, sorry," she replied as she looked up, then looked straight back down.

"No need to be sorry. I only know a few words in Russian."

"English is okay, I'm just a little nervous as I don't want to get anyone into trouble."

"That's fine. Just relax and tell me exactly what you saw." Placing the notepad on his lap, he clicked his pen, ready to write. She was the first person to call the hotline, so Blayze was eager to find out what she may have seen.

"I went out on the deck, near the casino, for a quick cigarette break around half past one-ish the day the girl went overboard. I saw Rachel as she walked right past me. She was heading to the front of the ship when a man, dressed all in black, came out of a door further up."

Blayze looked up at Maruska, catching her eye, and she quickly lowered her head again. "You're doing great. Did you hear anything?"

"He shouted something like 'How fucking could you?' and grabbed her arm, pulling her towards the door he had come out of. She pulled away from him and said, 'Don't you dare touch me again.'"

"What did this guy look like?"

"Slightly taller than her, white, long black hair with a bit of a beard. That's all I could see from where I was standing."

"That is very helpful, thank you. Did you see which way they went after that?"

"She pushed past him and went through that door and he followed. That's it."

"Maruska, that's been useful information that we didn't have. Now I need to find this man and ask him some questions." Blayze stood up, pen and pad in one hand, and shook Maruska's hand, which she took as her cue and stood too. He led her to the door, thanking her again, and showed her out.

He picked up his phone and called Ananda while sitting back at his desk. "Hey there, you guys have photos of everyone on board, don't you, from when they sign on and off?" he asked.

"Yes, we do," Ananda replied.

"Excellent. I'm on my way to your office now. I think we may have a potential suspect." He hung up the phone and, taking his pad with the guy's description on, headed up to the security office.

SIMON ARRIVED OUTSIDE Robert's cabin and tapped on the door while trying the handle. There was no answer, and his cabin was locked. He tried again and waited a little as he knew that the only time Robert locked his door was when he was on shore or in the shower. He waited for a few minutes, knowing that Robert must have heard his last knock as the crew member living next door to Robert answered, thinking it was for them. He took his cell phone out of his pocket and tried ringing the cabin, but there was no answer. Then he tried Robert's cell, and again, no answer. Simon looked down at his watch and noticed that it hadn't quite been fifteen minutes since Robert had called, so thought Robert may have nipped out for a coffee and would be back soon. He turned around and leaned back against the wall next to the cabin door when his phone went off.

"Simon, where are you?" Blayze said without even saying hello.

"Outside Robert's, but there's no answer."

"Stay there. I'll be there in two minutes."

Blayze arrived exactly two minutes later, yet there was still no sign of Robert.

"Everything okay?" Simon asked, pushing himself off the wall.

"I need to speak to you both, urgently. I think I know who is behind all of this."

"Holy shit, wow." Simon turned and tried knocking again. "Still no answer. I've been here nearly fifteen minutes now and there has been no sign of Robert at all."

"Let me try something," Blayze said, then pulled out his phone and dialled. "Hi, could you please put out a request over the ships tannoy for Robert, the cruise director, to call 0100 immediately? Thank you very much." Keeping his phone in his hand, awaiting a call, he looked back at Simon. "Let's see if that works."

They both waited for a few minutes, but no phone call came.

"Where the hell could he be?" Simon asked, now pacing the corridor.

"Give me a couple of minutes. Wait here." Blayze walked off down the long corridor and disappeared around the corner at the end.

Simon was now starting to get worried, especially after the recent days' events, and hammered as loudly as he could on Robert's cabin door. "Robert, are you in there?" He hit the door so hard that his hand stung. He stopped banging and rubbed his hand, feeling like he'd bruised a knuckle, then Blayze reappeared around the corner at the top of the corridor, followed by Antonio.

They reached the door and Simon stepped aside. Antonio pulled out a master key and placed it in the lock. While opening the door, Antonio banged and shouted for Robert. They entered and headed straight for the living room.

"That explains him not answering his phone," Blayze said, showing the others Robert's mobile, which he had found on the desk.

Simon checked the patio doors, which lead onto a balcony. "These are locked," he said, looking back at the others. He turned the latch and went outside. The strong wind sent the curtains flying, so he bounced back in and closed the doors. "Nothing out there," he added while the others continued to look around.

He watched Blayze and Antonio make their way into the bedroom and heard them rummaging through all of Robert's wardrobes, moving hanging clothes aside to search underneath them. Simon opened the bathroom door and turned on the light. As soon as he walked in, he fell backwards, smacking the door against the wall.

"What was that?" Antonio asked.

"Simon, are you okay?" Blayze shouted from the bedroom.

"Guys, you need to see this," said Simon, his voice hushed.

Blayze reached the bathroom first and saw Simon pinned to the door in complete shock. He looked towards the shower. "Shit." He let out an enormous sigh and was moved aside by Antonio, who wanted to see what Simon had found.

"Oh no, Robert," Antonio said. "How could someone do that?"

Robert was slumped in his shower, fully naked. They had tied his neck up, making it look like a hanging, but the blood dripping down his face made it obvious that this was no suicide. It was murder.

All three of them looked at the body in silence for a few moments until Blayze broke it by walking back towards Robert's desk. "Does anyone know where he keeps his camera?" He opened every drawer, then finally found it. "We need to take pictures for evidence before we move the body."

"Hang on. Did you say 'before we move the body'?" Simon asked after a couple of seconds, waiting for Blayze's statement to sink in.

"We can't leave him like this. The smell would attract attention."

"Let me call the doctor to see if there is space in the morgue," Antonio said, turning away from Robert's body and walking back towards the patio doors.

"Don't tell them who it's for, though. We will go down for the stretcher," Blayze added, before Antonio made the call.

Simon and Blayze returned from the infirmary ten minutes later with a stretcher and body-bag. They had told the doctor as little as possible. They had hoped to tell him even less, but he had insisted on knowing more before he just let any old body in the morgue without his knowledge. Blayze, now with a potential suspect in his head, knew it wasn't the doctor, but he didn't want information spreading so had sworn the doctor to secrecy about the deceased.

Antonio looked at Simon and reached into his pocket. "Simon, do me a favour. Here's my key. Please get me some more clothes. You'll find a small bag in the wardrobe on the left as soon as you walk in. Put them in there so no one sees them. If we intend on lifting Robert's body, I'm going to get covered in blood, and there's no hiding it when you're dressed all in white."

"Yes, sir." Simon took the key and left. He knew he would rather do that job than be lifting his dead friend into a body-bag.

SIMON WALKED ALONG the corridor to Antonio's cabin with his head down, still in a state of shock. He opened the door and went straight for the bedroom. He turned and slumped himself on the edge of the bed, throwing his head into his hands. Rocking back and forth and rubbing his face, he still couldn't get the image of Robert's hanging body out of his head.

Tears came streaming down his face. He grabbed a pillow, put it over his face, and let out an almighty scream, which was followed by even more tears as he sat and hugged the pillow for comfort.

"What the fuck is going on?" he questioned. "My last ever contract and this shit happens." He threw himself back on the bed and stared at the ceiling. "What's next?" he asked. "More importantly, who's next? Is it me? Is this how my life ends?" He closed his eyes and stretched his arms out to the sides, resembling a cross. "God, I know I'm not really a believer, but please, don't let me die like this."

Simon lay there for a few seconds, imagining how his family would feel, getting a phone call saying he'd been murdered on the ship, before sitting back up. Rubbing his hands up and down his face, he finally composed himself and remembered what he had been sent there for. He stood up and got Antonio's fresh, clean, white uniform out of his wardrobe and neatly folded it up. Taking out the bag that Antonio had mentioned, he placed the clothes inside. He put the pillow back in its place and brushed the quilt down, as he didn't want Antonio to know he had been lying on his bed.

Grabbing the bag of clothes, he headed towards the door, but stopped at the bathroom. He turned on the cold tap and splashed his face a few times with water, helping hide the tears and bringing him back to reality. After drying off, it was time to head back to Robert's cabin to see how the others were getting on.

BLAYZE STARTED TAKING pictures of Robert's body from all angles so he could share them with the authorities. Once finished, he placed the camera back on the desk and walked past Antonio who was just standing there, watching, having placed the body-bag on the bathroom floor. "Are you ready for this?" he asked.

"Not really, but what do you need me to do?"

"We have to release his neck first, without causing any more injuries, so I need you to get inside the shower and lift his body up slightly, so that the hose loosens."

Blayze could see that Antonio was nervous. "Just don't look at his face and you'll be fine."

Antonio walked into the shower and lifted Robert's body as Blayze released the hose from around his neck. Once it was loose, with Antonio still holding Robert's body under his arms, Blayze put his hands around Robert's ankles. "After three, we need to lift him carefully out of here and place him down, flat, on the bag."

Antonio looked directly into Blayze's eyes, ready for in-structions.

"One, two, three, up." They both lifted and felt the weight of Robert in their arms. Even though Robert wasn't a sizeable man, his body seemed to weigh a tonne. They placed his body on top of the bag and Antonio stood up to get out of the way. Blayze reached over and zipped the bag up part-way to cover up Robert's lower half and grabbed a close-by towel.

"Can you put some water on this?" Blayze asked, passing the towel over. Once Antonio had passed it back, he cleaned Robert's face so it was free of blood, and noticed the large head wound that had caused the amount of blood loss. "Have you seen this?"

"I think I've seen enough," Antonio replied while looking at the blood all over his uniform.

Blayze fastened the bag fully and used the same towel to wipe the blood off his hands. "One more lift," he said, looking up at Antonio. They lifted the bag onto the stretcher and fastened the buckles so the body was secure.

"How can you be so calm?" Antonio asked.

"This isn't the first body I've moved, and I doubt it will be my last."

Simon re-entered with a small bag of clothes for Antonio, who took them and went into Robert's bedroom to get changed. Blayze could tell that Simon had been crying by the redness of his eyes. "Who could have done this?" Simon asked, looking at the body laying in front of him.

"Let's get his body downstairs first, then we can all sit down and discuss what I've found," Blayze replied while pulling the trolley towards the door.

Antonio emerged from the bedroom, dressed in his pristine white uniform. "Are you both okay to take the body down and then meet me back in my office? We now have a serious problem with over two days left at sea before we reach Miami."

"We will be back up ASAP," replied Blayze, opening the cabin door. He looked down the corridor both ways to make sure no one was around before pulling the trolley out. It was only a short distance to the crew elevator, which they got in undetected.

SIMON HAD ASKED BLAYZE to be excused from the meeting with Antonio. Robert's body hanging there had had such an emotional effect on him that he couldn't think straight. Blayze had agreed and said he would catch him up later on all the findings and let him know how they would proceed. Wanting some time to himself, Simon knew of a spot on the open deck where hardly anyone went, so he could be alone with his thoughts. Having delivered Robert's body to the infirmary, he headed straight there.

The wind was powerful, but it didn't bother him as he knew others probably wouldn't brave being out there. The deck was wet from the rain that had fallen during a brief period earlier in the day, and where he was sitting was sheltered, so the sun had not yet dried it all up.

He sat there, trying to get the image of Robert's body out of his head, but he couldn't and broke down in tears. He sobbed for a while until the sadness eased off and reached straight for his cigarettes, realising it had been hours since he had last had one. There were only three left in the packet and, with the way he felt, he smoked them all back-to-back.

He stayed there for a little longer, alone with his thoughts, with the breeze in his face. After ten minutes, his phone rang. He looked at the number calling, hoping to be able to ignore it, but saw that it was Antonio, and didn't dare cancel the call.

"Simon. Blayze told me you needed some time, which I completely understand, but unfortunately time is what we don't have right now. I need you to make an announcement."

"Why me?"

"As dance captain, and with no cruise director or assistant cruise director, I need you to step up to the plate and take control of things for me," he said, asserting his authority as acting captain.

He wondered if he was capable at all, but, realising he had no choice, he took a deep breath. "What announcement do I need to make?"

"Have you seen the news about Hurricane Keelee?" After getting no response from Simon, he continued. "Well, they have upgraded her to a Category 4, and she is picking up speed. Although she is travelling away from us right now, she may switch and if that happens, we are heading right into her."

"Oh, fucking brilliant. Could this day get worse?" Simon asked.

"I need you to be the voice for this one and to keep people calm. I know you can do it."

Simon knew he was just saying that to make him feel better, but he had no choice. "I'll do my best."

"Pop up to my office now and I'll give you a spare key for Robert's cabin. That way you can use his intercom from now on."

"But, sir—"

"Listen, don't worry. We've cleaned the room; you can feel safe in there. Just make sure you lock the door behind you when you are in there alone."

Now worried and more nervous about stepping back into the room after a murder had taken place there, Simon hesitantly agreed to see him in his office after a quick visit to the shop. He needed more cigarettes.

CHAPTER TEN

On his way to the shops, Simon passed the sports bar, where the news was playing on the TV. Everyone in the busy bar was watching the screen. Simon thought it would be best to see what he was dealing with. And there it was: the predicted trajectory of Hurricane Keelee. "Oh shit," he uttered, forgetting where he was.

"Gonna be a big one, they say," said a middle-aged American man, sipping a Bud Light and staring at the screen.

"Sure is," Simon replied, quickly heading off before the man had time to turn and recognise him as a crew member. He continued to walk through the ship and reached the vast array of shops selling clothes, jewellery, liquor, souvenirs, sweets, and various other luxuries. They were busy; with it being another sea day, people had nothing to do but spend. And the more deals the shops put on, the more passengers flocked. Today's deal was on clothing and jewellery, so the queue for the cigarettes in the liquor shop was short. Being polite, he let everyone there go in front of him; frankly he was happy if someone else turned up as that stalled him from having to go into Robert's cabin, but then his turn came.

"Is everything okay, Simon?" asked Chelsea from behind the counter.

"Yeah, fine. And you?" Simon replied, putting on a smile. He knew Chelsea, but only from crew parties and the odd drink in the crew bar. Not exactly a friend you'd spill your se-crets to.

"Is that everything?"

"You know what, let me get a bottle of Absolut too. Think I may need a good drink later." He reached back to the shelf near the counter and got a bottle.

"Why not," she said, taking it out of his hands, scanning it and putting it straight into a bag.

Simon paid for his items and began to leave.

"See you in the bar later?" Chelsea asked.

"Maybe not tonight; I've got this to go through instead," he replied, lifting the bag up in the air.

"True. Catch you soon."

Simon left with a wave of his free hand and headed to An-tonio's office to collect Robert's cabin key.

BLAYZE WAS SITTING on a bar stool in the far corner of the poolside bar, near the window. He had ordered a double whisky; something to clear his mind and help him focus. The bar wasn't busy. There was a young couple at the other end sip-ping Long Island Iced Teas, and the odd customer would come over for their next round of drinks. The pool was closed for the time-being as it was very windy, causing water to splash all over the deck. Thus everyone up there was sitting around the edges, under the ship's coverings, shielding from the wind.

It was almost time for the first teatime sitting, and Blayze noticed it had become much quieter around him. "Another one, please," he said, raising his hand towards the bartender.

"Coming right up, sir," came the reply from across the way. As the bartender placed the drink in front of him, she looked at him inquisitively. "Now I remember who you are." There was a slight pause as she briefly closed her eyes. "Blayze, wasn't it?"

"Yeah, that's right."

"How's the investigation going? Any news about the captain yet?"

"Can't really talk about it up here, just in case," he said, quickly making sure there were no ears close-by.

"Oops, sorry. Never thought. I'll leave you to it."

"Great, thanks." And with a nod, the bartender left and carried on with her duties.

The 'ding dong' of an announcement about to happen came over the ship's tannoy and Blayze spun his seat around to face the pool, as the speakers were by the stage area. He leaned one arm on the bar, still holding his glass. "I wonder what this is about," he said to himself out loud, thinking no one was around.

"Probably about meal times and tonight's entertainment," the bartender said, appearing right behind him.

"Jesus Christ!" Blayze jumped around in shock. "You were just over there a second ago." He gestured to the other side of the bar.

"Need to be quick in this job," she replied with a cheeky wink.

"Bloody hell, any need." Shaking his head, he turned back towards the pool.

"Good evening, ladies and gentlemen, this is your dance captain, Simon, here."

Blayze tilted his head in thought. "He sounds calm, that's good," he murmured to himself, so as not to get another shock from the ninja bartender behind him.

"I just wanted to give you a little update on tonight's activities. I'm sure some of you know that there is a storm nearby. Please rest assured that we are watching it closely."

"A storm?" remarked a passenger who had just walked up to the bar. "Who's he kidding? It's a fucking hurricane!" The passenger, in his late sixties, was wearing beige pants, a bright Hawaiian shirt and a fedora. He seemed very relaxed despite the fact he had mentioned it was a hurricane. "Why can't they just say what it is?"

"Because of this, we have moved tomorrow night's live show, Caribbean Wonders, to tonight. The show times are..."

The passenger turned and looked at Blayze. "Grand excuse to watch sexy ladies in next to nothing dance around at the wife's choice, hey?"

"Yeah. Look, but don't touch, right?" Blayze replied, pandering to the filthy mind of the dirty old man.

"You got it."

"...and the second seating will start at eight o'clock. We will regularly update you all on the storm's position. Thank you, and enjoy your evening."

"Excuse me, sir, did that guy say it's a hurricane?" the girl from the young couple at the other side of the bar asked.

Blayze looked over and realised she was asking him, so he spun back around to face the bar. He stalled for a second, trying to think if he should reiterate what Simon had just said. "Well, it erm, well, yeah, it is. I can't lie to you. I saw it on CNN earlier." He thought he had better not say he had heard it from the staff captain, as to them, he was just another passenger.

"Holy shit!" she exclaimed, worriedly. "How far away from it are we, do you know?" His answer hadn't helped, as Blayze then saw the panic in the girl's face.

"Don't worry, we must be a sufficient distance away from it," he said, trying to ease her mind. "They would have told us otherwise."

Suddenly the bartender piped in. "We're not far away from it, actually. It's just on the other side of the island we've just passed."

Blayze glared right at her.

"Is that right?" the girl asked.

"Yeah, but it's heading the other way. We will be fine," Blayze said, now trying to divert the conversation. "Did you guys enjoy Antigua?" Unfortunately, his attempt at changing the conversation didn't work as the couple got up from their stools.

"We need to tell your mom and dad," the guy said to his girlfriend. Turning back to Blayze, he continued. "Sorry, sir. Nice to meet you, but we have to go. Her mom and dad don't do well in storms."

"No worries. You take care and please don't worry. Everything will be okay." His reassurance wasn't received as they had already walked away by the time he had finished speaking.

He looked back to the bartender. "Seriously?" He shook his head in disbelief as he put his drink down on the bar and stood. "What a way to cause panic."

"It just slipped out," she replied apologetically, shrugging her shoulders while continuing to clean a glass.

"Who knows what else has slipped out? For fuck's sake."

SIMON WAS BACKSTAGE early, getting ready for the 'Caribbean Wonders' show. He wanted to get all of his costumes ready before going over the new spacing for the show, now that Rachel and Tammy were no longer in it. He had worked it out the previous night and had posted the changes on the dancers' board so that they could be prepared. Luckily the two girls were opposite each other on stage most of the time so it had made most of the changes pretty simple; it was just the occasional partner changes that had needed to be altered to make it look good.

Both Rachel and Tammy had shared the same dressing room as Simon and the other boys, which meant there were two empty spots on the counter, making the room feel empty yet giving them more space. As much as Simon wanted to spread out and utilise the vacant areas, he couldn't bring himself to put anything in their places. He was just finishing putting his last costume on the bench when David popped his head into the dressing room.

"Hey, so does this mean we get tomorrow night off, then?" David asked.

"Hey, man, how's things? It looks like it. If this hurricane heads towards us, we wouldn't be able to do anything, anyway."

"Excellent," David replied and began to leave.

"Did Blayze catch you yet?" Simon asked.

David turned around and walked into the room towards Simon. "What do you mean by that?"

"Oh, he mentioned that he needed to ask everyone about their relationships with Rachel, and I heard that you two had a thing a few years back."

"Well, no, he hasn't, and that's the past, anyway. Better leaving the past where it belongs, don't you think?"

Simon noticed that David's tone of voice had changed and thought it best to leave the questioning to Blayze. "Yeah, I do. Don't want my past being dug up; all those skeletons in the closet, hey?" he jested, trying to brighten the mood.

"Exactly. Well, I'd better go and get the pit ready and warm up," David said, walking away.

Simon looked up in the mirror in front of him and, as David reached the door, he turned and looked Simon right in the eyes. There was a split-second where neither of them spoke, and they both froze.

"Drinks afterwards?" David asked, breaking the silence.

"Sure." Simon watched as David left.

He shook his head, rubbed his face with both hands and looked at himself in the mirror. "That was weird," he said to himself, recalling the change in David's tone and demeanour when he had mentioned Blayze and Rachel. Shrugging it off, he carried on getting ready. As a few more dancers arrived, Simon nipped upstairs and onto the crew deck for his pre-show cigarette. His phone rang, and he noticed it was Blayze.

"Hey, Blayze, how's everything going?"

"Where are you right now?"

"Crew deck having a quick smoke before warm-up in twenty minutes."

"Stay right there. I need to tell you something important."

"Okay, see you—" Before he could finish, Blayze had already hung up. "Well, that's nice," Simon said to himself, putting the phone back in his pocket. He took a seat and waited for Blayze to arrive, wondering what could be so urgent.

A few minutes later, Blayze burst through the door. "There you are! Over here, quick!" He gestured for Simon to follow him to a spot where no one would be able to hear them, even though the deck was empty. "I need to tell you what we found earlier."

"Okay, go on," Simon replied, eager to hear the update.

"We had a witness come forward, saying that Rachel was last seen arguing with a man out on the deck near the casino before they disappeared inside. This was only minutes before she went overboard."

"Do you know who it is?"

"The description she gave was superb, and with Ananda's help we were able to find someone who fit it perfectly. You're not gonna like it, though." Blayze shook his head.

"Just tell me." Simon's voice rose, wanting Blayze to just spit it out.

"It's David Pennington, the musical director."

Simon stepped back in shock. "Are you sure?"

"One hundred per cent. He matches who the witness saw with Rachel."

"That still doesn't mean it's him, though, right?" Then Simon recalled how David's mood had changed when he asked if Blayze had caught him yet. His shock turned to realisation.

"Well, no, but we need to question him ASAP as he is our only lead. I need you to think about everything you know of him so I can be prepared."

"Yeah, I will, but I've got a show to do right now. And so has he." Simon looked down at his watch. "I need to head to the stage as warm-up is about to begin." He went to walk away but was stopped by Blayze grabbing his arm.

"Whatever you do, be careful. If it was him, he may have murdered Alice, Tammy and Robert, too. We don't know what we are dealing with here."

Simon looked back in sheer worry. "Shit." Blayze let go of Simon's arm. "Let me do the show, then afterwards I'll sit down and write everything I can."

"Cheers. And er, hey, break a leg."

Simon headed in and, upon reaching the backstage entrance, he bumped into a handful of musicians hanging around in the hallway.

"You okay?" David asked. "You look like you've seen a ghost."

Simon looked directly into David's eyes, now wondering if he could be a stone-cold killer. Making up an excuse, Simon replied, "Yeah, just didn't feel too well and was sick a little." He carried on walking past them when David stopped him.

"You look after yourself. We don't need another man down."

Simon didn't know where to look. He just wanted to get away. "See you on the stage, everyone," he shouted, and continued past them.

As he entered backstage, he thought to himself, 'What does he mean, another man down?' But he brushed off the comment as soon as he entered the dressing room. It was show time, and that had to be his focus.

As the show began, thoughts of what Blayze had just said to him started flooding back. His concentration was all over the place. He had forgotten that in the middle of one of the songs, there was a long instrumental section that featured the band. While that happened, the band pit lifted and moved to the back of the stage, bringing them into the show. As soon as Simon stepped back on to the stage after that section, he felt David's eyes on his back, making him uncomfortable and causing him to make countless mistakes. That was not like Simon at all, but he just couldn't shake off the feeling and suddenly ran off stage in the middle of the routine and darted for the dressing room.

He reached his spot and dropped to the floor in tears. Once the number had finished, Andrew rushed in. "Simon! Is everything okay?"

Simon, with his head in his hands, covering the tears, replied, "I'm not feeling well at all." He jumped up and ran to the toilet to be sick. The overthinking and worry that a friend of his could have caused such tragic deaths had taken its toll on his body. He slumped over the toilet seat, unable to stand.

"Don't worry, the show is nearly over and we can finish it without you. I'll tell everyone now," Andrew said and ran out.

Simon, didn't want anyone else to see him like this, so he picked his body up and got out of his costume. Leaving everything on the side, he headed to his cabin.

Once back in his cabin, he locked the door and sprawled out on the bed, distraught at what had just happened. He had never had to run off stage like that before, but he just couldn't continue. He could still picture David's eyes glaring at him, the image churning his stomach again.

After waiting a while and letting his body settle, he phoned backstage to speak to Andrew. He asked him to apologise to everyone for him and to let them know he was feeling a little better now. He also asked him to put his costumes away as he hadn't had a chance earlier. He knew Andrew would understand as Simon had done the same for him before.

After hanging up, he grabbed some water and lay on the bed, staring at the ceiling with his mind still racing. There was no chance he was going to able to sleep tonight with a potential killer in the next cabin.

CHAPTER ELEVEN

Blayze finished his breakfast and walked through the atrium. He glanced out of the windows to his left as he passed the elevators and noticed the sea was still rough. He knew this meant the wind would still be strong outside, but he wanted a bit of fresh air, regardless. He looked up and saw that an elevator was on its way down, so waited for it alongside an elderly couple.

"Good morning, dear," the old lady said to Blayze as he approached them.

"Good morning, ma'am, are you having an enjoyable time?"

"Ooh yes, this is our third time on this ship. We love it, don't we, dear?" She turned to her husband for acknowledgement.

"We couldn't pass up the chance to see some different islands, now, could we?" her husband replied. "Shame we had to miss one."

The elevator arrived, and Blayze let the old couple enter before him.

"Thank you, sir," the man said.

"No problem. Which deck are you going to?" Blayze asked after pressing Deck 7 for himself.

"Eight, please," the lady replied. "Is this your first cruise, young man?"

"I've been on a couple before, but mainly for work purposes. This is my first one off duty."

"Well, I hope you are enjoying yourself and not thinking about work. What is your position on board?" she asked.

Realising what he had just said, Blayze tried to think of a position that would only need to visit now and then. His mind was so focussed on the case that he had forgotten who he was talking to. "I'm from..." he paused to think of something quickly, "...head office." Just as he had finished speaking, the elevator stopped at Deck 7 and he stepped out. "Have a lovely day, both of you," he turned and said. The pair waved back as the doors closed.

After a brief walk down to the aft of the ship, Blayze arrived at the coffee shop and stopped to look at the menu.

"Can I help you, sir?" the staff member behind the counter asked.

"A large caramel latte, please, with an extra shot." Knowing it could be an interminable day, he thought there was no reason not to get the extra caffeine.

The girl passed his order onto her colleague, who was waiting by the coffee machine, while she took the next order. Blayze moved along to the end of the counter to await his coffee. He looked around and noticed there was an empty table and chairs just opposite the counter, right by the window. His coffee arrived, and he took a seat.

He pulled out his phone, wanting to call Simon to see how he was after having told him about David the night before. The phone rang, and at first there was no answer. He waited a few minutes while starting his coffee and gazing out onto the open ocean before trying again. This time he got through.

"Sorry, Blayze, I was in the shower," Simon answered before Blayze could even say 'good morning'.

"That's okay, I just wanted to see how you were after the show last night."

"After what you said, I couldn't bring myself to go to the bar so I just went straight back to my cabin and locked the door."

"Well, I will speak to David later on this morning and find out about his relationship with Rachel, and ask why he was seen arguing with her that day. I'll piece that together first, before asking his whereabouts after the get-together at the beach in Antigua."

"Please let me know what you find out. He lives right next door to me, so I've kept the shower running while on the phone, just in case he is listening. But I can't keep doing that every time the phone rings."

"Hey, listen. Why don't you, for the time-being, only use your cabin for work — so people see you still going in there — but use Robert's old cabin to sleep in? No one will know you are there and you don't have to tell anyone."

"You know what, I will do that. It'll be easier for these morning announcements than having to wake up and keep going up and down all the time. Cheers, Blayze."

"No problem. Listen, I'll catch you later on with any updates, okay?"

"Thank you," Simon replied and Blayze hung up.

Blayze sat there for a little while longer, finishing his coffee, when the girl from behind the counter came over and stood next to him.

"Sorry to bother you, sir, I forgot to ask you before at the counter. Did you find the captain?"

Blayze looked up at her in shock, then slowly lowered his head in utter shame that she could say something so stupid in earshot of everyone. It wasn't like she had whispered it, either; it was at full volume and had unfortunately caught the ear of a portly middle-aged man sitting at the next table reading a newspaper.

"Did you just say 'find the captain'?" the man asked the server.

Then, without thinking or even taking Blayze's facial expressions on board, she turned and said, "he's been missing for a couple of days, now."

"What?!" the man replied. "We have no captain, and he's missing? Missing where? Where is he?" The man got louder and louder, attracting the attention of other passers-by who had made their way over. Blayze looked around and noticed more and more coming over to hear what the man was shouting about. Not wanting to give up who he was just yet, as that would rouse more suspicion, he knew his best option was to get up and leave before the man could question him as to why the server had asked about finding the captain.

He quickly grabbed his coffee and sneaked past the crowd, which was getting bigger by the minute. Unfortunately for the young female server, she was now in the thick of it, being questioned from every side and trying to wriggle away.

Quickly reaching for his phone, he called Antonio. "We have a problem."

ANTONIO HAD CALLED Simon and Ananda to his office, knowing that Blayze was on his way up. Blayze had arrived first and had already told him about what had happened at the coffee shop before the other two arrived. Once they were all in his office, Antonio filled them in. "We now have three problems."

"Three?" Blayze questioned.

"To catch you two up," Antonio said, looking at Simon and Ananda, "a waitress at the coffee bar has let slip that the captain is missing, so we need to get in front of that as soon as possible to stop it spreading further."

"I knew it would come out eventually," Simon added.

"Our second problem is catching the killer. Are we any closer to that, Blayze?" Antonio leaned towards him, hoping for some pleasant news.

"I'm still working on it. I'm questioning our lead suspect straight after this meeting, so I will know more in a couple of hours."

"Excellent. Now comes our third problem. We have received news that Hurricane Keelee is now heading our way. She changed course just an hour ago and we are sailing straight towards her. She is picking up speed, and is expected to become a Category 5 by the time we reach her." He looked around at the three people in front of him and waited for a response, yet the expression on their faces said it all. "We are trying to plot a course that will take us away from her, but if she picks up speed, we won't make it in time."

"I've just had a thought," Simon said, stepping closer to the desk. "As no one has seen or heard from the captain in a few days, they probably would not recognise his voice. With you both being Italian, you," he said to Antonio, "could pretend to be him and be the voice from the bridge during this time, and I will still be the face people can come to."

"Actually, that's a superb idea," Blayze said, smiling up at Simon.

"I get one or two now and then," he jokingly remarked back.

Looking back towards Antonio, Blayze added, "But don't make an announcement just yet. Wait until I've spoken to David so that it doesn't disrupt my questioning."

"So, problem one solved. You, sir, are pretending to be the voice of Captain Argenti, correct?" Ananda asked to make sure he had that right. "Problem two is still ongoing."

"Correct, but I may need your help, depending on how it all goes," Blayze replied.

"Problem three: still to come. I think I've got it all now. I will get my staff to secure things right away, to save time later."

"Thanks, Ananda," Antonio said, sitting back in his chair. "We've got a lot ahead of us and we still have another full sea day after this. Blayze, call me after your questioning and I will make my first announcement, apologising for not being around as I've been unwell. Simon, I need you to put together a plan of activities for today, to make adjustments for the weather, and some for tomorrow. Let's get ahead of this thing." He stood up to let them all know the meeting was over. "Thank you, everyone, and stay safe."

He shook their hands from behind his desk, thanking each one of them again individually, Blayze being last. "Get the bastard who did this."

"I will, sir, I promise."

SITTING IN BLAYZE'S cabin was David, ready for questioning. Blayze noticed that David seemed very relaxed and even had a smug look, like he was prepared for whatever was to be thrown at him. Blayze was sitting on his bed, again with his notepad and pen, ready to fill in any information that he didn't already have.

"So, David, thanks for coming to see me. I'm sure you know what this is about by now."

"My relationship with Rachel, I presume." David sat with his arms folded, slumped in the desk chair.

"Correct, yes. Now then, can you tell me a little more about it, please?"

"I don't know what you want me to say, really. We dated a few years back, and that was it."

Blayze noted that David's attitude towards his questioning was very blasé. It was going to take some prying to get anything out of him. "When was this?"

"I don't know, about four years ago, maybe? A lot has happened since then. I can't keep track of everyone I've slept with, can you?"

"Well, no. But if an ex of mine had been murdered, I would want to give as much information as possible to clear my name."

Blayze's reply threw David a little, and he unfolded his arms. "You told us all she went overboard. I presumed she just jumped."

"Her injuries tell us otherwise." Blayze paused to get a re-action from David, but he just looked directly at him with no emotion at all. "Therefore, we are asking everyone who knew her for as many details as possible, so we can try to figure out what happened."

"Don't know what I can tell you, really. She was my ex, and that's about it," he said, re-folding his arms.

This was going to be tougher than he thought, so Blayze went all-in with the hope of catching the reaction he wanted. "You were one of the last people to see her alive. We have a wit-ness that puts you with her just minutes before she was seen going overboard." He waited for a response which never came. "Can you confirm you saw Rachel that day?"

"Yeah, I saw her briefly, but it was a quick conversation and I left."

"What were you arguing about?"

"We weren't arguing. She had ignored me the night before and I wanted to know what her problem was, that's all."

"So when someone ignores you, you grab them by the arm and try to drag them aside, do you?"

"I hardly touched her," David snapped back, sitting upright in his chair. Blayze noted down David's immediate reaction as he seemed defensive. "I wanted a private word, away from any-one else, and asked her to come inside with me. Dragged her, huh? I don't know who your witness is, but they have it all wrong."

"That's why you're here; to set the story straight. And I appreciate it." Blayze knew he had something here but still needed more information.

"How much longer is this going to take? Don't you have everything you need, now?" David asked, looking eager to leave. He sat forward, ready to push himself up from the chair.

"I just have a few more questions, then you can get back to what you were doing."

"Shoot."

"Can you remember why your relationship ended?"

"I don't know. Probably the end of a contract, like most relationships do on ships."

"Is this the first time you've worked together since then?"

"Yeah, it had been a while since we had seen each other. We bumped into each other once, a year and a bit back in Cozumel, but we didn't say much as we were with our own crews at the time."

"Did you know Captain Argenti?"

"What's he got to do with this? I thought you wanted to know about Rachel."

Knowing by the tone of David's voice that he had hit a sore spot, Blayze continued. "Well, you know they were lovers, don't you? They had been on and off for years, by the sound of it."

"Well, you can ask him that, if you ever find him."

"Do you know where he could have gone?" Blayze asked, as David's previous comment had sounded suspicious.

"No idea. Who knows what a captain gets up to, hey?"

"Was he your captain when you and Rachel were together?" Blayze was trying everything he could to squeeze just something out of him.

"I don't know. Never met the captain back then. Had nothing to do with him."

"Would it make a difference to know that he *was* the captain back then, and they had possibly started seeing each other while you two were together?"

"She wasn't like that back then. Not like she was before she died. I believe she had turned into a right slut. Glad I had nothing to do with her."

"Just one more question before I let you go. After the beach get-together, where did you go?"

"Erm, I came straight back to the ship," David said hesitantly.

"Okay, so you spent all day at the beach, correct?" Blayze knew he was lying as he had got a taxi back with some others, who had arrived back on the ship a couple of hours earlier.

"Yeah, and came straight back on board."

"That's great. Thank you so much for coming to see me. If I have any further questions, I'll let you know." David stood up, ready to leave, and walked towards the door. Blayze held out his hand and David shook it.

"You've been extremely helpful. Thanks again," Blayze said as he opened the door.

David didn't say anything and just walked out. Blayze closed the door behind him and sat back at his desk to make a call to the doctor.

"Hey, Doctor, Blayze here. Can you forward a copy of Rachel Lawson's medical file to me via email, please? There's something I need to check out."

"Give me ten minutes and I'll email it to you when I get back to my office," the doctor replied.

"Can you send me David Pennington's too, please, while you're at it?"

Blayze knew that David wasn't telling him everything about their relationship, and that there had to be more to it.

"Yes, of course. They will be with you shortly."

As soon as Blayze put the phone down, he called Simon. "Simon, can you come to mine, now, please? I need to ask you a few more questions."

"On my way," replied Simon.

Simon arrived just as Blayze received the email from the doctor with both of the medical files he had requested. "Thanks for coming by. Is there anything about Rachel's history, that you know of, which may cause David to be angry with her?"

Simon perched on the edge of Blayze's bed. "Nothing that I can think of, why?"

"There was something not right about the way David reacted when I mentioned that Captain Argenti was on the same ship as him when he was dating Rachel. When I said that her affair may have started then, his whole demeanour changed. He wasn't telling me everything."

"I didn't know them back then, I'm sorry."

"That's okay, I just thought I'd ask in case you had heard anything in passing."

The room went silent for a moment as Blayze continued to read David's file on his laptop. "Oh, hang on a minute. Did you know David was on antidepressants?"

"I had no idea. How long has he been on them?"

"Well, it doesn't say he's on them at the moment, but he has a history of needing them from time to time."

"I wonder when he started taking them."

"That's something we need to find out. Whether it is Rachel-related is the question. Has seeing her again brought something back up which may have caused him to snap? Simon, do me a favour. I need you to ask all your cast members if they know about Rachel's past and if she was hiding anything. This could all be linked, somehow."

"I'm on it," Simon replied, standing up.

Blayze turned around to look at him. "We may be dealing with a very unstable man here who could fly off the edge at any moment, so please be vigilant around him and question with caution."

"Don't worry, I'll be careful."

As Simon left, Blayze carried on reading the rest of David's file.

CHAPTER TWELVE

"Nws just in. In a sudden change in direction, Hurricane Keelee, which has now become a Category 5 hurricane, has moved west and is now on course to hit the Bahamas within a matter of hours. This new trajectory will see it touch land on Florida's south coast as early as mid-morning on Saturday..."

Simon turned off his TV as he didn't need to hear any more. The news bulletin had just confirmed what Antonio had said, and now anyone keeping track of the hurricane would know that they were heading right into its path. His hands became clammy as his mind began to imagine what could happen. Even though he had plenty of experience of storms, he had never headed directly into the path of a hurricane before. He'd only ever brushed by one which caused everyone on board — both crew and passengers — to panic. That near miss had damaged almost all the stock in the gift shops, and he knew this would be worse. This was going to be an unknown experience altogether.

While on his way back from Blayze's cabin, he had called Lisa, who was Rachel's cabin-mate. On paper, that was, anyway. Lisa spent most of the time with her boyfriend, Colin, the Shore Excursion Manager, leaving Rachel to have the cabin all to herself. Simon had asked her to collect all of Rachel's belongings and bring them to his cabin for safekeeping until they

145

reached Miami. That was what he had told her, anyway. The actual reason was so he could have a good rummage through everything for clues as to why David would have wanted her dead.

The sound of suitcase wheels rolling along the floor and bouncing off the metal strips where the fire doors were got louder and louder, and he knew it would be her. He opened his door and peered into the corridor, and there was Lisa, on her way down. He waved to let her know he was in, then heard another door open between them. A head popped out.

"Who's making that racket?" David asked while looking both ways, first clocking Simon, then Lisa.

"Sorry, mate, it's my fault," replied Simon with an apologetic wave of acknowledgement. "I'm just storing some things in mine for the time-being."

"I'd just got my head down too."

"Again, mate, I am sorry. You know, though, that we have to get everything tied down and secure ASAP, don't you?" Simon wondered if David had even heard about the hurricane.

"Oh, for fuck's sake. This day just gets better and better." David looked displeased.

"Oh, well, that's nice! Hello to you, too!" Lisa said as she made her way past David's door.

"Not you," David replied, staring right at her. "I've had enough of this shit already. Anyway, you're packed up early, ain't ya? You don't leave for a few more weeks." He noticed the two suitcases and a large bag that Lisa had pushed and pulled along the corridor.

She slowed down slightly to talk to David. "It's all Rachel's things. Simon asked me to pack them up and bring them round." Simon waved to usher her to get a move on.

"Cool." David watched her continue to the next door, all the while keeping an eye on the luggage.

Lisa reached Simon's door, and he helped lift the cases into his room. "My God! What's in these?"

"Heavy, right?"

"You're telling me," Simon replied, lifting the first case onto his bed. As Simon reached out to get the remaining bag by the door, he clocked David still watching him and hurried inside with it. Once he had lifted it onto his bed, next to the two suitcases, he turned back towards the door. "Thanks, Lisa. I appreciate your help."

"Anytime, sweetie," she replied and walked away, leaving the door open.

Simon quickly went to close the door when David appeared. "Jesus, man, you scared me!" Simon put his hand to his chest and took a deep breath.

"Have you got all of Rachel's things in there?" David questioned, peering over Simon's shoulder.

"Yeah, packed and ready to be sent back to her family." Simon didn't want to let David near any of it and had to come up with an excuse to quickly get away. "I need to dash upstairs to make an announcement." Squeezing past David, who was still staring at Rachel's luggage, Simon closed the door and locked it.

"Don't normally lock your door, do you?" David asked.

"Well," Simon replied hesitantly. "Someone else's belongings are in there now, too, so I need to look after them, don't

I?" He scurried away, wanting to distance himself as much as he could. "Don't forget to tie everything down. It's going to be a big storm, this one."

"It certainly is," David muttered, and walked back to his cabin.

Simon waited around the corner for a few seconds until he heard David close his door. He sneaked down to where he had just come from and slowly placed his key in his lock so that it wouldn't make a sound. He did everything in slow motion, despite the noise of the waves crashing against his porthole being loud enough to cover any sound he did make.

The waves had become bigger over the past hour, and the thud of the ship as it crashed down on the water was like clockwork. Simon knew that if he timed it well, he would be able to open both suitcases to see what was inside without David hearing him through the wall.

The first thud came. He sat and counted the seconds between the second and third thuds and noticed a pattern. "Perfect," he whispered, and proceeded to open both cases. It took longer than normal, but these were not normal conditions. With a potential killer on the other side of the wall, silence was key.

He searched through everything carefully and placed a few things that he thought could be of interest to Blayze to one side. Not wanting to talk on the phone, he emailed Blayze and asked him to come and collect everything, but to be quiet and careful as David was in his cabin next door, and he didn't know Simon was back in his. Simon sat there in silence, unable to do anything now except wait for Blayze. He watched the waves crashing at his porthole. This sight usually made him calm, but the odd sound from David moving next door made him anxious.

Almost thirty minutes later, without knocking, Blayze entered Simon's cabin. "Hey, man, what have you found?" he whispered, keeping his volume to a minimum.

"There are a couple of airmail letters from her family and a photo album of people I don't know. I presume they must be relatives, but I'm not sure." He handed them to Blayze, who glanced through them. Simon waited to see if Blayze spotted anything.

"I'll take these with me and see what I can find. Is he still in there?" Blayze tilted his head towards the wall between Simon and David's cabins.

"I think so. The TV is still on and I haven't heard him leave."

"Okay. Let's get out of here before he realises that you've returned."

Simon went to open the door, being as careful as possible not to make a sound. He let Blayze exit first so he could lock it behind them. Blayze stood next to him, keeping watch, but just as he pulled the key out, David emerged from his cabin and spotted them. He looked at them both, then at the items in Blayze's hands.

"Hey, mate, are you off upstairs to secure everything?" Simon asked, re-entering his key to make it seem as if they were coming, not going.

"Yeah." David glanced at Blayze, looked down at the items, then back at Simon. "You'd had better do the same," he added, making direct eye contact with Simon.

"I'll be up there shortly," Simon replied, turning the key and opening the door. Simon entered, but Blayze stayed where he was, watching David walk away. When David reached the end of the corridor, he peered back over his shoulder, noticing Blayze still standing there, watching him. He paused for a second, then left.

"He knows something's up, I can just tell," Blayze said, returning his focus towards Simon, who was in the doorway in his cabin.

"Shit."

"You need to secure everything backstage, ready for the hurricane, so I will have a look through these. If I were you, though, I would wait until David has finished before going back there."

BEARING IN MIND BLAYZE'S recommendation, Simon wanted to delay going backstage for a while, in case David was there. As a big lover of storms, Simon wanted to catch a glimpse of Hurricane Keelee before they closed all the doors and the ship went watertight. So he took the opportunity to head to the crew deck at the bow of the ship for a cigarette. He pushed the door, which seemed ten times heavier than normal because of the powerful wind. Outside, the sheets of heavy rain bounced off the deck in front of him. "Fucking hell," he muttered to himself.

"You're telling me," came a voice from around the corner.

Simon tentatively stepped around to see who it was, trying not to get wet. "Hey, Andrew, have you come to have a look too?" His friend was hiding in a little alcove, having a cigarette, and Simon went over.

"I've come for my last fag until this is over. We won't be allowed out until it's safe."

"Shit, yeah. I'd not thought of that. I'd better get a couple in now, myself." He reached into his pocket and pulled out his smokes. The wind was so strong that he had to use Andrew's body as a cover to light his cigarette. "This is going to be one hell of a storm," he stated. "The last storm I went through smashed up the gift shop. Everything had been thrown off the shelves, there were smashed bottles everywhere, and booze was pouring down into the atrium like a waterfall."

"I'm surprised you didn't stand underneath it with a glass to catch it all," remarked Andrew.

"Cheeky git. It was the middle of the night and I was fast asleep throughout it all. You know me, my head hits the pillow and I'm out."

There was a chill in the air due to the amount of rain pouring down, which had blown onto the pair of them throughout their conversation. The sky had become a grey mist and they could hardly see past the ship.

"Hey, have you heard anything from Tammy and Alice?" Andrew questioned. "Are they safe?" This threw Simon a little as no one had mentioned them for a while.

"The last I heard, they would meet us back in Miami," he replied, trying to remember the story that he, Blayze, Antonio, and Ananda had come up with.

They were had to shout as the wind had picked up and was whistling past them.

"It's just that I tried messaging Tammy, but I've had nothing back."

"She may be in the air on her way, ahead of this storm," Simon quickly responded.

"I doubt it. I looked online this morning, and they have cancelled all flights to and from anywhere in this area."

"I really can't tell you any more. That's the last I heard." Simon realised that sooner or later the truth would have to come out and he would have to tell all his friends he had been lying to them. Keeping little secrets was one thing, but lying about friends and colleagues having been murdered was completely different.

Simon stepped away, partly to break up the conversation, but also because he was desperate to get a better view of the storm approaching. Holding onto a post for security, he peered over the side of the ship to see what they were about to encounter. He had only stepped out of the alcove for ten seconds, but he was already soaked from head to toe. He didn't care, though, as the sight in front of him was too good to miss. The grey mist cleared ahead, revealing dark clouds looming in the distance, like a desert sandstorm rolling its way over the ocean. The sight of lightning bolts just ahead told him that they were near the edge of the storm. "Andrew, come and see this!" he yelled over his shoulder.

"I'm not getting soaked, you can bugger off."

"It's your loss."

"That's what windows are for, didn't you know? Anyway, I'm off in before it gets worse."

"Okay, see you later," Simon said, not losing his focus on the lightning show right ahead. Bolts were jumping from cloud to cloud, with the occasional full sheet lighting up the entire sky.

He stayed there for a few minutes, getting wetter and wetter. Then a sudden immense crack of thunder came from right above him. "Holy fuck!" he shouted. "This is amazing!" Unfortunately, his time outside was about to be up. A security officer had appeared to usher him indoors as they were about to make the ship watertight. Reluctantly, Simon had no choice but to go inside. Leaving a trail of water behind him, he knew he had a spare change of clothes and a towel backstage. He headed for the changing room, still thinking about the view he had just seen, completely forgetting who was already back there.

CHAPTER THIRTEEN

Sitting on his bed with papers all around him, Blayze started reading the letters from Rachel's family. Most of them were about generic family business like what they had been up to recently, especially the letters from her parents. Blayze had been able to get their names from Rachel's social media platforms, as they had liked almost every photo she had ever uploaded. A couple of the letters were from her sister, which was easy enough to see as she had signed them all off 'Love your big sis xx'. In all of them, she mentioned how 'Little J' was doing, how she was growing and crawling around the house. Was this Rachel's niece they kept talking about?

Opening the photo album, Blayze saw pictures of a husband and wife at their wedding, with all of their family around them. Seeing Rachel next to the bride, he assumed that it must have been her big sister's wedding. Carrying on through the album, he noticed the couple holding a baby girl in their arms. 'That answers that question,' he thought, writing the fresh information down on his sheet.

Wanting to know more about her sister, he opened up Rachel's laptop and went straight to her Facebook page. Looking at the list of her family members, she only had one name next to 'sister', so he clicked to open her profile. After going through her photos online, Blayze knew it was her, alright. The pictures of the baby were identical to some in the photo album. He scrolled back through her photos, seeing the child get younger and younger, reaching the day of the first photo of her. "Hang on a minute," he uttered to himself while looking through dates on the sheets surrounding him. He continued through a few more photos, and something didn't add up. Rachel's sister didn't have any pictures of her being pregnant or at the hospital. 'Did they adopt?' he thought. It was a possibility.

Looking back at Rachel's profile, he headed to the time that the baby should have arrived. But there was nothing. In fact, there wasn't anything between when she had finished her contract that year, and when she returned to work, on her next ship, which was twelve months later. How was she missing a year? Going back and forth between her mum's and sister's profiles for that same year, there wasn't a mention of her. Not even a single photo. It was like she had disappeared off the face of the planet. Blayze cross-referenced the dates and discovered that Rachel had gone dark the year after she and David had been together. Soon after they had broke up and parted ways, she had cut ties with the world.

Was the break-up worse than David had mentioned? Was it so bad that she'd had to come off everything? Was he stalking her and her family? Blayze couldn't find the answers to these questions without confronting David again.

As Blayze picked the photo album up once more to see if he had missed anything else, it slipped out of his hand and fell onto the floor. A couple of the pictures that had been back-to-back had fallen. "Shit," he said to himself, having to shuffle off the bed to pick them up. "Wait a minute."

He picked them up to find writing on the back of each of them. 'Love you, mum', said one, and the other said, 'Love you, J'. Taking out the rest of the pictures, Blayze noticed that all of them had writing on. After reading them all, he realised that Little J was in fact Rachel's daughter, not her big sister's, and that she had kept her a secret from everyone.

The big question now, though, was who the father is. Is it David? Or Captain Argenti? The timing suggested that it was one of those two, and with what had happened so far, it looked like David may have found out the truth.

DAVID WAS IN THE STORAGE room, taking down instruments from the shelves, placing them on the floor so that nothing could fall off and break during the storm. He heard someone enter backstage and walk towards the dressing room. He turned around and noticed that it was Simon, who was soaking wet and had his head down, so hadn't seen him.

David turned back and continued what he was doing to make sure everything was safe from potential damage before locking the room back up. He knew that Simon had been talking to Blayze and had given him some of Rachel's belongings, but how much did he really know?

Walking towards the dressing room, he saw that Simon had left the door open. This was his chance to find out. He crept towards the door and could only see the top of Simon's head behind a rail of clothes. Waiting for his moment, David sneaked in and hid behind the open door.

He stood there for a while, remembering what he had done to the girls for talking to Blayze, and what he would have to do to Simon if he had said anything. At this point, there was no turning back. It had gone too far. He needed the element of surprise to catch him off-guard, though, as Simon already knew that he would be up here.

He peered around the door to see what he was up to. He noticed that Simon had got changed and was putting his clothes in the washing machine. He had to be careful as the door was still open, therefore he didn't want him to scream. He waited patiently, fingers tapping at his side, ready for the opportune moment to strike.

SIMON HAD STRIPPED off his wet clothes and was drying himself with a towel he had grabbed from the laundry room, which was in the far corner of the dressing room. He reached down to the shelf below the counter in front of him and pulled up a bag containing his rehearsal gear. He always kept it up there in case he ever ran late.

After putting on his jogging pants and a clean pair of socks from his drawer, he put his wet clothes into the washing machine and set the cycle going. Knowing exactly how long the washing would take, Simon started taking down all the head pieces with the girls' costumes on, plus anything else he could find, off the top shelf. There was plenty to keep him busy, as the shelf ran along the full length of the mirror, which covered two walls of the dressing room.

He had just placed the last piece of costume on the floor when the dressing room door slammed shut and David appeared. "What the fuck?" shouted Simon. "How long have you been there?"

David walked towards him, not saying a word, backing Simon up against the counter on the far wall. "What do you know?"

"I don't know what you mean," Simon said, shaking his head, breathing faster and faster.

"How much do you know?" David asked again, this time with much more anger in his voice and rage across his face. He waved his finger in Simon's face. "Don't fucking lie to me, Simon. I saw you with that Blayze bloke holding Rachel's belongings."

"I swear, I don't know anything. He took them with him." Simon held both hands up in defence. Right at that moment, Simon's phone rang.

"Don't answer that," David said forcefully.

"What if it's important?"

"What, more important than right now? I very much doubt that."

The sound of his voice made Simon realise that he wasn't messing around, and that if he didn't play this well, it could be the end. "Okay, okay. I won't."

"What has Blayze got on me?"

"I don't know."

Sick of hearing the same reply to everything he asked, David cupped his hand around Simon's throat and pushed him onto the counter. He forced Simon into a horizontal position, and exuded anger and rage. He squeezed his hand tightly around Simon's neck, closing off his airways.

Simon panicked, and grabbed hold of David's hand to force it back, but his attacker was strong.

"Just fucking tell me!" David yelled.

"I'm telling you the truth," Simon squeezed out.

The commotion inside the dressing room had caught the attention of Tony, the stage manager, who had come backstage to strap up the scenery. He burst through the door and David instantly released his grip.

"What's going on?" Tony asked, shocked at what he saw.

"Just a misunderstanding," David replied. "Nothing for you to worry about." He walked away from Simon and pushed past Tony, leaving the room.

Tony rushed over to tend to Simon, who was attempting to get up. Simon rubbed his throat to get some circulation back to it.

"What the hell went on there?" asked Tony, helping Simon stand up. "Are you okay?"

"I must have said the wrong thing at the wrong time." Simon didn't want to say too much. "He's grieving for Rachel more than I thought." He started picking up all the hats that had been knocked over in the struggle. "Don't worry, I will sort it out later once he's calmed down. I need to get a move on, there's so much to get off the shelves in here and in the other dressing room. Thanks, Tony."

"As long as you're okay." Tony placed a comforting hand on Simon's shoulder.

"Yeah, I will be. Let's get cracking before something breaks."

Tony exited the room, leaving the door open. Simon picked everything back up and looked at himself in the mirror. He could see David's finger-marks on his neck. "He left his mark there," he said to himself, then remembered his phone had rung earlier. Getting it out, he noticed it was Blayze, so called back.

"Simon, I've got news. I need to speak to David again. It looks like there's a baby involved."

"What?"

"Too much to go through over the phone, but have you seen David?"

"You've just missed him, actually. He just had his hands around my throat wanting to find out what I know, and what you have on him."

"Are you okay?"

Simon rubbed his neck once more and let out a deep breath. "Thankfully, yeah. Our stage manager arrived just in time. David's a lot stronger than he looks, I'll tell you that."

"If you see him anywhere, call me straight away."

"Will do."

"Be careful. He's attacked you once and will do it again if he sees you."

"I'll be keeping my distance, that's for sure."

"I'll fill you in on everything later when I see you. Must see if I can find him."

Blayze hung up and Simon continued making everything in the dressing rooms secure before locking it all away.

ANTONIO HAD RECENTLY made an announcement, telling all on board that the ship would reach the edge of the hurricane within the hour. Everyone was to remain away from the windows and avoid walking around the ship wherever possible. He had explained that the crew had been around and left seasickness bags outside every cabin door, and all external doors that lead to deck areas had been sealed shut and were out of bounds. The ship had gone on lockdown for everyone's safety.

Knowing that the ship would be clear of almost all passengers — except the ones who thought that because they had paid for the cruise, everything had to remain open just for them — Simon headed from backstage towards Deck 7 to meet Blayze. He walked through the theatre towards the mid-ship stairwell. It felt like constantly walking uphill and downhill as the ship rose and fell among the high waves. The smell down the corridor was already unpleasant thanks to all those who had been sick and not made it to a bathroom in time.

He reached the stairs and held on tight to the banister, using it to pull himself up. He had to take the stairs as all the elevators were now out of order, in case the ship lost power because of the storm. Reaching Deck 7, Simon made his way past the shops, which he noticed had already suffered some damage. Rails of clothes were on the floor, along with broken glass from shelves that had fallen down.

Seeing the odd passenger attempt to walk in a straight line while the ship was moving how it was always brought a smile to Simon's face. They looked like they had been out on the town all night, staggering from side to side and bouncing off everything in their path, like they were stuck in a pinball machine.

Carrying on a little further, Simon reached the coffee shop, where he found Blayze waiting for him.

"I asked you to meet me here, one, because I know you love your storms, and with a view like that, you wouldn't resist." He gestured to the window. "And two, because it is quiet, so I can tell you what I've discovered."

"I like your thinking," Simon replied.

Noticing the bruising that had appeared on Simon's neck, Blayze reached towards him and pulled down his collar. "He grabbed you tight, then?"

"That was with only one hand."

The smashing of cups falling out of the cupboard behind the coffee shop interrupted them.

"Listen, I appreciate your help in all of this," Blayze began. "You know these guys better than I do, and I'm sorry you've had to lose a few friends along the way." He put his hand on Simon's shoulder. "But it's not over yet. We still have to catch him before he does anything else. Do you know of any places around the ship that David usually goes to?"

"Apart from the crew bar and his work places, I don't really see him out and about."

Blayze placed a file on the table in front of Simon. "In here is everything I have, and I think I know what got David started on the antidepressants. I got hold of Rachel's mum again to ask her some more questions. It seems like, as far as David was aware, Rachel terminated her pregnancy as soon as she got home, killing his baby."

"Well, that would send anyone off the rails. Especially if he didn't have a say in it."

"Exactly."

The ship suddenly became extremely dull as the ominous cloud Simon had seen looming earlier was now on top of them. The ship's internal lights were already on, but the darkness outside made them feel much dimmer than usual. Thunder roared around them and flashes of lightning captured Simon's attention. "Sorry, Blayze, I've always wanted to be a storm chaser and now I'm in one. It's fantastic."

Simon was excited, but the look on Blayze's face was one of someone who wasn't fazed by anything. It was no wonder people were drawn to him and he was so good at his job. He could look death in the face and not care, and yet still look hot doing it.

Simon dragged his attention away from the window and read the file Blayze had given him. "Wow, there's a lot of stuff in here. You've been busy."

"That's part of my job." While Simon kept reading, Blayze pulled out his phone and made a call. With the phone to his ear, he looked at Simon, who glanced up at him. "Still no answer."

"Is that David you're trying?"

"Yeah. He's either ignoring my calls or he's staying away from his cabin, as it would be too obvious a place to hide."

"I would agree with the latter, to be honest."

"Well, now we know who we are up against, but we don't know what state of mind he is in. If we don't catch him soon and get him medicated, things could become a lot worse before we reach Miami."

Simon closed the file and placed it on the table. "What do you suggest we do?" He was eager to help. He didn't want to lose any more of his friends and was willing to do anything to stop David.

"Well, right now, the storm is working to our advantage. Everyone is in their cabins and staying safe. Safety is our foremost priority, but we need to do a sweep of the ship to find him."

"I can help with that."

"I will get hold of Ananda and Antonio and let them know, as they can help, too. But no one else. The fewer people out and about, the better. Since it is only us who know what has really happened, it will cause less panic."

Blayze made the necessary phone calls while Simon turned to continue watching the storm. The waves were enormous, and it was no wonder the ship was nose-diving over them just to stay afloat. The best way was to head into the wave, because if they were side-on, a gigantic surge could knock them over, and that would be it.

Once Blayze had finished his calls, he put his phone back in his pocket. "We have a plan. The four of us will split up, with two at the bow and two at the stern and we will comb the ship deck by deck. One of each pair will start at the top, and the other one at the bottom, each time meeting in the middle. We will cover more ground that way. Ananda is going to get us all walkie-talkies so that we can communicate with each other. We need to head to the security office now, to pick them up."

"Excellent plan. Lead the way," Simon said with excitement. As much as this was dangerous and he could be putting his life at risk, it thrilled him to be a part of something that he had only ever seen in a movie.

They hurried towards the security office where the search would begin. "Simon, I can't tell you how much I need you to be careful. Remember, he was your friend first, and he may use that to get close to you. Whatever you do, don't be a hero."

CHAPTER FOURTEEN

The hurricane threw the ship about as if it was a mere rowing boat. The only things that could be heard were the creaking of metal, the crashing of items falling down and the screams of terror coming from distant cabins. There were flashes of light as the ship crashed on the waves, causing power-outages makin it difficult to see at times.

In their search for David, Antonio and Ananda had agreed to start from the lower decks, with Blayze and Simon from the upper decks. They each started at one end of the ship and met at the halfway point before doubling back on themselves, then moving up or down. That way they could be certain they hadn't missed anything. Each deck was taking some time to search as they tirelessly tried to keep upright and keep moving.

All except Blayze were nervous as they would be alone during the search, and didn't know how they would react if they ran into David. The state of mind David was in, anything could happen. Blayze had warned them all before starting that if they saw even a glimpse of him, they should not engage, but instead they should radio the others, with their location, and they would all meet there.

Antonio was heading up the staircase at the aft of the ship, gripping the banister with all his might so as not to fall backwards. He had just hauled himself to the top step when a crew member, who was on his way down, appeared from around the corner. Already on edge, Antonio jumped back in fright, barely stopping himself from losing his footing on the step.

"Can I get by?" asked the crew member. Antonio just stood there, holding his chest with one hand, trying to catch his breath. Without saying a word, Antonio waved the guy past him.

Antonio pulled himself back up from the railing and stepped onto the I95. "Vaffanculo," he uttered as he breathed a sigh of relief. He carried on walking down the I95 and met Ananda in the middle, right next to the crew mess hall. "Am I glad to see you."

"Are you okay, sir?" Ananda asked, looking worried and exhausted.

"I am now. Have you spotted him yet?"

"Not yet, sir."

"Right. Let's head back and move up. Remember, from now on, we'll be on passenger levels, so make the search look natural."

"Yes, sir."

They parted and cautiously walked back in the same direction from which they had come, again looking along each corridor. Antonio was still calming down from the shock but knew he had no choice but to carry on. He rested against the wall, pausing for a moment to compose himself and relax his pulsating heart before continuing his search.

SIMON AND BLAYZE MET at the centre of Deck 9. They had moved down the decks quite quickly as many of the higher decks were open air and all the weather-tight and external doors had already been closed. No one would dare brave going outside as the wind was so powerful that they would be blown straight overboard. Antonio had also told them that under no circumstances should they open an external door, even if they see David outside. It was for everyone's safety, as well as their own.

The last thing on Simon's mind right now was venturing outside. As much as the storm still looked amazing, he was thankful that he could see it from the warmth of inside the ship. He remembered what it was like trying to keep his eye on Rachel the day she went overboard. The swell of the ocean then was nothing like it was right now. There would be no way anyone could survive out there if they fell, and he knew it. There wasn't much to search on Deck 9 — mainly just passenger cabins — so Simon and Blayze quickly reached the stairwell in the middle of the deck.

"Anything down your end?" Blayze asked.

"Still nothing." Simon shook his head.

Blayze turned away and spoke into the radio. "Anything from the lower decks?"

"Negative," replied Antonio.

"Nothing yet, Blayze. Up top?" asked Ananda.

"Negative. Let's keep moving." Blayze clipped the radio onto the side of his pants and turned towards Simon. "What's on the next deck?"

"Same as this one. It's Deck 7 which may take us a little longer."

"Okay. Let's head back up and get the next one done. It shouldn't take long as there aren't any places to hide when it's just one long corridor."

"See you down there shortly."

"Stay safe." Blayze smacked Simon on the side of the shoulder, as he had done every time they had met in the middle, to remind Simon not to lose focus. Simon was pleased he had been partnered with Blayze, as he felt safer and calmer around him.

Just as they were about to part, they heard Antonio on their radios.

"Blayze, come in."

"Blayze here."

"We need to re-evaluate how we search Decks 5, 6 and 7. There is just too much for one person."

"Okay. Let's all head to the purser's desk in the atrium and reassess."

WHEN THEY REACHED THE atrium, Blayze was shocked at the damage the storm had already caused. The black, baby-grand piano, which had been sitting on a small stage at the rear of the elevators, was now in the middle of the floor, on its back. Various chairs from different parts of the atrium were scattered all over the place, and still moved around every time the ship listed from side to side. The cables securing the large chandelier, which hung from the decks above, had snapped. The once majestic centrepiece was now swinging in a circular motion like a pendulum, narrowly avoiding clattering into the atrium's outer walls.

"Let's not stand anywhere near that, in case the whole thing snaps and lands on us," Blayze said, ushering the group to the other side of the elevators and out of harm's way. Just as they got there the ship listed again, throwing them against the elevator doors. The air was filled with a cacophonous crash directly above their heads. The chandelier had smashed into a glass panel on one of the upper decks and shards of glass were falling like daggers all around them. They huddled together and, as a group, made a run for it, away from the elevator and towards the theatre doors.

Once away from the immediate danger of falling glass, they took a second to catch their breath.

"That was a close one," Blayze stated.

"These decks have so many places to hide," said Antonio. "I suggest we all stick on the same deck and work our way through each one from front to back."

"Agreed," replied Blayze. "Let's stay in our pairs and split left and right."

"We'll take port and you guys take starboard," Antonio decided.

They made their way through the theatre doors and across the auditorium floor. Once on stage, they split to their respective sides and resumed their search, heading backstage to begin. After discovering nothing there, they made their way onto the stage and were just about to walk down into the auditorium when they all heard a snap, which sounded like the breaking of wood. Quickly turning around, Blayze noticed that a piece of scenery and broken loose from its straps and was heading straight for them. The brakes on the wheels had come loose from being knocked around and it was hurtling down, picking up speed. "Quick, get off the stage!" Blayze shouted, and they all made a panicked dash for it. Within moments of them reaching the auditorium floor, the set piece nose-dived fifteen feet into the band pit at the front of the stage, smashing into multiple segments as it hit the bottom.

"That's that show cancelled for a while, then," Simon surmised, looking down into the pit, shocked at what he could see.

"We need to move on," Blayze said, looking at them all. "Let's go,"

Searching the theatre took longer than expected, and Antonio had been right to get them all together. One person looking between every row of seats would have taken the same time it took to search two full decks. They finally finished and headed back into the atrium.

Simon looked at Blayze. "We have to do all that again."

"What do you mean?" Blayze questioned, a puzzled look across his face.

"When we get back onto Deck 6. There's the theatre circle to look through and it has the same amount of seats as the stalls, but they're tiered, so it may take even longer than that did."

"Brilliant," Blayze replied. He did not look pleased.

The search continued with each pair on their respective side, occasionally having to split up if there was more than one avenue to lead them through. Deck 5 didn't produce anything, and on Deck 6 there was still no sign of David.

"Last deck," Blayze said, and they headed up to Deck 7. Time was running out, and as the hours had passed while searching, so had the storm. They could feel the movement of the ship under their feet beginning to become calmer. It was almost dawn, and they knew that soon, people would wake and start venturing around the ship again. As they reached the end of Deck 7, Blayze could see how tired Simon and Ananda were from their faces, but it was the look of frustration from Antonio that worried him. They had finished their search empty-handed. David was nowhere to be found.

"Guys, we tried, but he is obviously much cleverer than we thought," Blayze began. "The only thing I can think of is that he may be hidden away in someone's cabin. It will be much harder to find him once the ship becomes functional again, as we will have thousands of people around us."

Antonio looked through a nearby window and noticed the first of the sun's rays peeking over the horizon. "Let's all get some rest and we will continue to look later in the morning. Thank you, all, for your help."

"Pass me your radios and I will put them back on charge for later," Ananda said, holding out his hand. Once each person had handed over their radio, Ananda slowly headed back to his office.

"I'm going to my office, too," Antonio said, "to find out how much damage this hurricane has caused. Then I will make the morning announcement before getting a few hours' sleep. I recommend you guys rest now, too, so we can search again before lunch." Antonio walked away, leaving Blayze looking at Simon.

Blayze could tell that the adrenaline had worn off as Simon looked exhausted. "I will call you in a few hours, okay? Lock your door, remember," he warned Simon. They separated and headed to their cabins, knowing David was still out there. Somewhere.

THE CREW HAD BEEN AWOKEN early as there was a lot of work to be done to make the passenger areas safe. Glass needed swept up, furniture had to be rearranged, liquids that had showered the halls had to be mopped up, and the chandelier had to be secured. Blayze had been unable to sleep and was wandering around the ship, watching the crew work hard to clean up the mess Hurricane Keelee has caused.

As he passed by the sports bar, someone had turned the TV back on. A news bulletin was giving an update on the storm. It showed that once the hurricane had reached the Bahamas, it had been downgraded to Category 3 and moved north, with the eye of the storm now heading for Jacksonville. They had been lucky.

If it had continued on its original path, there would have been no escape. Unfortunately, the pictures on the screen displayed the devastating effect that Hurricane Keelee had caused in the Bahamas. She had destroyed entire villages, leaving many homeless and causing numerous fatalities.

As far as Blayze knew, no one on the ship was injured, but the stench in the air made it clear that there had been a lot of seasickness. Although the sea was still choppy, the crew had reopened the weather-tight doors. Someone had also pushed the doors on the main decks open to let the smell of vomit and alcohol out and the fresh air in.

The worst affected area he encountered on his walk around the ship was the shopping mall. There were so many smashed objects lying all over the floor that it was difficult to tell one from the next. Only the odd bottle of booze was left standing on the shelves, and the manikins in the shop windows looked like they had just been thrown over in a pile as if they were junk.

An announcement from Antonio came over the ship's tannoy, asking passengers not to venture out of their cabins just yet, because the clean-up was still in progress. He also gave an update on the whereabouts of the hurricane.

This hadn't stopped some people from already coming out to take pictures of the mess the ship was in. Something to post back home, to boast that they had survived, or to moan about how the ship looked, to try to get their money back. People would do anything for a refund these days, and the crew had been there and seen it all before, so they were well-prepared for the blame of a natural disaster.

What shocked Blayze was the end of Antonio's announcement. "Finally, I ask for David Pennington, the musical director, to contact security as soon as possible. Thank you, all, for your understanding, and I will let you know when it is safe to leave your cabins."

'Why would you do that?' Blayze thought to himself. Now, not only did all the crew know David's full name and position, but so did all the passengers. Plus, everyone was now aware that security was looking for him. Too many people asking questions could lead to David panicking and doing something completely reckless.

Quickly reaching for his phone, Blayze called Antonio. "Why did you do that?" Without waiting for a response, he carried on. "This is only going to get worse, now, and it's on your head."

"Excuse me? I'm now the captain of this ship." Antonio replied abruptly. "I intend to flush him out by whatever means necessary."

Blayze dropped the phone to his side. "Fucking idiot," he said, scratching his head. He lifted the phone back up to his ear. "You need to be ready for what you may have caused here. You are tired and not thinking straight, and you should have gone through me, first, before outing him like that for the entire ship to hear. I can guarantee that wherever he was hiding last night, he won't be there now."

"Well, I suggest you start your search again and let me know when you find him." The phone went dead as Antonio hung up.

"What a fucking idiot! Aarrgh!" Blayze screamed at the phone. He was met by some strange looks from passengers, who he had not seen until he turned around. Realising where he was, he carried on walking until he found a quiet section of the ship. He called Simon and told him what Antonio had just said. Simon explained that he could get that way sometimes. One minute, he's a pleasant guy, and the next, he's on a power trip. "Brilliant. We've a murderer on the loose, and now Captain Arrogant in charge. This should be fun."

"Hang on a second," Simon whispered hastily. "I can hear movement next door. In David's cabin."

"Wait right there. I'm on my way." Blayze hung up and ran down the nearest staircase he could find, rushing toward the crew deck. Pushing past anyone in his way, he had to get there fast.

CHAPTER FIFTEEN

David had stayed in Tatiana's cabin all night. She was a waitress, and was one of his go-to girls no one knew about. They had spent the night together some time ago after one of the monthly crew parties, and had hooked up on several occasions since. He knew he could hide there for as long as he needed. He heard Antonio's announcement while still lying in her bed. Upon hearing his name, he panicked and quickly jumped up and got dressed.

"Why does security need to see you?" Tatiana asked, rolling over and watching him get ready.

"It doesn't matter," he brushed off. "Go back to sleep. It's nothing."

She rolled back over. "Fine. Whatever. See you when you next need a piece of ass to take your mind off things."

Ignoring her comment, he finished getting ready and left her cabin, silently closing the door. As he turned the corner he spotted Blayze walking towards him, looking down the next corridor. David quickly jumped back so as not to be seen and dashed back into Tatiana's cabin. He waited in there for five minutes before sneaking out again.

When he reached the end of the hallway, he peeked around the corner and noticed Blayze had moved further down. Once Blayze was a good distance away, David dashed across the corridor, crept up the stairs and headed into passenger area. He was wearing the jeans and T-shirt which he had deliberately changed into the night before, so that his usual all-black outfit he wore in the band pit wouldn't give him away. Being dressed like this meant that he could blend in with the passengers and stand a better chance of avoiding detection.

More and more passengers were now exiting their cabins and heading for breakfast, so he tagged along, avoiding any eye contact with the crew members he passed, who were finishing cleaning up the mess from the hurricane. Looking at the atrium floor from a few decks above, he noticed that the piano had been flipped over. That was something he really should have been worried about, but right now, he didn't care at all. Instead of stopping to investigate, he made his way to the Lido deck, where a buffet-style breakfast had been prepared. He joined the long queue and heard people chatting about the storm, but they seemed happy and glad it was all over. After making small talk with other passengers who were standing in front of him, he helped himself to a plateful of sausage, bacon, egg and beans. He asked the people he had been talking to if he could join them on their table. They agreed and, with his back towards the pool, he hid in plain sight.

BLAYZE REACHED THE end of Simon's corridor and saw him standing in his doorway, looking nervously at the cabin next door.

"Someone is still in there, I can hear them," Simon whispered, gesturing for Blayze to get there quickly.

Blayze rushed past Simon and reached David's door. He paused for a second to take a deep breath. Poised ready with his side against the door, he turned the handle and flung the door open. "Freeze!" he shouted.

Simon rushed in behind Blayze, only to notice Ananda standing there, going through all of David's belongings. Ananda jumped back in shock.

"What the hell? I thought you were David," Simon said. "You had me all worried that he was right next door."

"Ananda, what's going on?" Blayze questioned.

"I had my orders to search through all of David's things."

"And what if he had come back and found you here on your own? What then, hey?"

"Antonio wanted it doing right away. I don't know what he was expecting me to find."

Blayze looked at them both. "Listen, guys, Antonio is doing more harm than good right now. If he gives you an order, I need to know right away." Simon and Ananda both nodded in agreement. "Him outing David like that to the whole ship will cause him to panic and act irrationally. We should reach Miami in the early hours of the morning, so that only gives us today to catch him." Blayze walked towards the door. "I suggest we get out of his cabin now and find him. Let's get to work."

"Where should we go?" Simon asked.

"You take the front, Simon. Ananda, you take the middle, and I'll take the stern. We'll search from bottom to top. Time to move."

ANDREW WAS ON THE LIDO deck stage setting up for the morning breakfast quiz he had been asked to do. After turning the microphone on and announcing that the quiz would begin in ten minutes' time, he reached into the bag he had brought with him for pens and paper. He wasn't looking his usual well-groomed self, as he had not had much sleep through the storm and a lot of his beauty products had smashed in the bathroom.

He made his way around the tables to hand out answer sheets and, to his surprise, spotted David sitting with a group of passengers.

"What are you doing up here?" Andrew asked David, who he noticed wasn't wearing his name tag.

Everyone else around the table stopped eating and looked at David, wondering how Andrew knew him.

"Just grabbing some breakfast," David replied, looking Andrew right in the face. "Is that the answer sheet? Brill." David snatched one from Andrew's hand and placed it on the table. He turned to face the people he was sitting with and immediately changed the subject. "What a storm that was, hey, guys."

This threw Andrew and he didn't know how to respond. He walked away, shocked at the way David was acting, and headed back to the stage to begin the quiz. He read out the questions and answers, all the time glancing over at David, who looked like he was just enjoying the moment, oblivious to the fact that he shouldn't be there. Crew could not take part in activities like this as it would be seen as cheating, and yet he was sitting there, with no name tag on, acting like a passenger.

Once the game had finished, Andrew went back around the tables to collect in the paper and pens. When he reached the table where David was sitting, David stood up and shook his hand.

"Good quiz, we came close."

Andrew couldn't figure out why David was acting this way. He was pretending not to know him at all. "My pleasure, sir," Andrew said, attempting to go along with his façade, despite not understanding it.

David walked away, so Andrew quickly went back to the stage and grabbed his gear, wanting to catch up with him. He followed him towards the gym. 'Where's he off to?' Andrew thought. He watched David go into the male changing room and followed him in. As soon as he got through the changing room door he was met with a punch in the gut, making him drop everything that he had been carrying.

"Why are you following me?" David asked as Andrew keeled over in agony. "People need to stop following me." David picked Andrew up by the scruff of his neck and threw him further into the changing room, locking the door behind him. Andrew crashed into the lockers at the other side of the room and fell to the floor.

"Why is security after you?" Andrew asked in fear as David made his way toward him. His hands were shaking with nerves and he could see the rage in David's face. "Has it got something to do with Rachel?" With a swift kick to the chest, Andrew was down again.

"That bitch had it coming, the lying piece of shit." With that, David kicked Andrew again, who curled himself into a ball.

"You're the one who threw Rachel overboard?" Andrew hid behind his arms, trying to protect his face.

David reached down and picked Andrew up. He grabbed him with both hands and pinned Andrew against the lockers. "You have no idea." He leaned in closer to whisper in Andrew's ear. "With the captain gone, she should have been all mine."

Quivering with sheer dread, Andrew asked, "Did you kill the captain, too?"

David's eyes, now only centimetres away from Andrew's, had pure evil in them. "The other two, well, that was their fault, really. They shouldn't have been speaking to him."

"What other two? And who?" Andrew asked, confused by what he was talking about.

"Who knows what they said to him? But I couldn't let them live."

"Who are you talking about?"

David released his grip and paced around, leaving Andrew where he was, relieved to have been let go of. "They knew too much, I'm sure of it. They knew about me and Rachel and they told that cop everything." He wasn't even talking to Andrew, he was talking to himself.

"I still don't know who you're on about!" Andrew was still baffled by what he was saying.

David rushed back towards him and pinned him against the lockers once more. "Alice and Tammy, Alice and Tammy, Alice and Tammy!" David seemed to be repeating it so that Andrew wouldn't ask again.

"Wait a minute, Simon said they were meeting us back in Miami."

"Yeah, well, they're not. He lied to you. He's known since that day as that Blayze fellow found them."

Andrew felt his rage come from nowhere and he forced David back into the wall. "You killed my friends!" He shoved him again. "You bastard."

DAVID REALISED THAT Andrew knew too much and wasn't prepared to let him go now. He rugby tackled him to the ground and pinned him to the floor.

"Get off me, you evil piece of shit!" Andrew yelled.

David immediately covered Andrew's mouth and punched him in the stomach, winding him. He released his hand and grabbed Andrew's head at both sides. He lifted it off the ground and pounded it into the floor four times, getting harder with each downward movement.

Although Andrew was now lying there unconscious, David hadn't finished. His fists came hurtling down from either side onto Andrew's face, turning it from right to left constantly. He kept going until his face was unrecognisable. Blood was spattered all over the walls and lockers, but David didn't care and he wasn't done yet. He needed to make sure Andrew would never speak again.

Standing up, David walked over to where Andrew had dropped his quiz equipment earlier and picked up a pen. He took the ink out of the plastic tube and went back over to Andrew's body. "Say goodnight, dickhead." He stabbed the plastic tube into Andrew's neck, hitting the major artery. Blood poured everywhere.

David sat on top of Andrew for a short while, looking at what he had done, then stood up and grabbed one of Andrew's arms. Dragging him across the floor, David opened the door to the sauna and shoved Andrew's lifeless body inside, turning up the heat as he left. That would give him time to get away before anyone spotted him.

He headed towards the sink and turned on the tap, eager to wash Andrew's blood from his hands and face. His clothes were covered with Andrew's blood, but he didn't care. He looked at himself in the mirror, water dripping off his face. "Who's next?"

CHAPTER SIXTEEN

B layze stood at the stern of the ship, leaning on the railing and looking out on the vast ocean. While contemplating his next move, his phone rang. Seeing who was calling, he wasn't too keen to answer, but thought it best that he did. "Antonio, how can I help you?"

"Blayze, he's struck again."

"What?! I told you this would happen."

"I know, I know. Listen, it's another cast member."

"Who is it?"

"Andrew Hinde."

There was a moment of silence from both of them. "Does Simon know yet?" Blayze asked.

"Not yet. Andrew's only just been identified. The worst part, though, is that a passenger found him."

"Oh, shit. This will get out of control soon, and right now, we need calm." Blayze began walking back towards the door. "I'll call Simon now and get him to meet us in your office."

"Okay. I'll call Ananda and get him up here, too."

Blayze hung up and immediately called Simon. "Hey, man. Listen, I've got some terrible news."

"What's up?" Simon asked.

"Andrew Hinde has been found dead. I'm so sorry." Blayze could hear Simon burst into tears at the news. "I know you're upset, but I need you to come to Antonio's office right away."

Blayze heard Simon sniffling, then blowing his nose. He sounded very choked up, but agreed and ended the call.

"I'M SO SORRY, SIMON," Antonio said, placing his hand on Simon's shoulder in sympathy.

Simon couldn't speak. Someone he trusted had brutally murdered three of his dancers. His friends. He was in utter shock that it was happening.

"We've got some even more unwelcome news," Blayze began. "It was a passenger who found Andrew's body."

"How? Where was he found?"

"They found his body in the sauna, up in the spa," Ananda said, walking into Simon's view from by the door. "By the bloodstains on the ground, it looks as though the murder happened in the male changing room, then the body was dragged into the sauna."

"How could someone do that?" Simon couldn't believe what he was hearing.

"Well, now we know that David is becoming extremely irrational," Blayze added. "Leaving blood everywhere means he's lost the care to clean up after himself, which shows that he is reckless and unsteady."

Antonio leaned forward on his desk. "Do you mean you believe he will strike again?"

"Without a doubt. Unless we catch him within the next few hours, more blood will be spilt."

Hearing this response, Simon leaned forward and put his shaking head in his hands. "Please, no. No one else."

"What do you need us to do?" Ananda asked Blayze.

"I feel this is all my fault," Antonio said, sitting back in his chair.

Blayze threw him a look, agreeing with him, which Simon caught sight of. "Never mind that now. We need to get everyone back in their cabins without causing too much of a panic."

"But how?" asked Antonio.

"What about Noro?" Simon suggested.

"What?" Blayze asked.

"Let's use the last resort you mentioned the other day, now that we know our killer. Announce that the ship must go into quarantine because of Norovirus. It's happened on ships before. We don't allow anyone out of their cabins until it is clear."

"I forgot about that. Let's do it." Blayze tapped Simon on the back. "Let's get the doctor in on this now, and if anyone asks, it's already spread. Make an announcement as soon as the doctor is up to speed. Ananda, once the announcement is over, I need your team to usher everyone back to their rooms. Everyone apart from the engine and bridge staff, that is, as we still need to get to Miami on time. Simon, come with me. We'll go to the security office and see if we can spot any signs of David's whereabouts on the surveillance cameras."

ANTONIO GOT OFF THE phone to the doctor. He had explained the recent events and had told him that if anyone asked, he already had thirty cases so far, with numbers increasing.

He composed himself and hit the intercom button. "Good afternoon, ladies and gentlemen, this is your captain speaking. Unfortunately, we have some terrible news. Although we have only just reopened the ship, having cleared up after the storm, we now have to close everything once more. We have received news that the ship has cases of Norovirus, so we must enforce a full lockdown in order to contain the spread of this virus. This means that everyone must now head back to their cabins until further notice. Food and water will be brought to all cabins in due course. We apologise for this news, and hope you understand that your health and safety are at the forefront of every decision that we make. Please make your way to your cabins, now. Thank you." Antonio looked over at Ananda, who was waiting for him to finish. "Empty those decks."

"Yes, sir."

SIMON AND BLAYZE WERE sitting in the security office, watching the many monitors on the wall. With the aid of a joystick and a control panel, they were able to select various cameras all across the ship and move them in whichever direction they required. Until now, all they had seen were security guards, still ushering passengers to their cabins. The odd few passengers had been reluctant to move, but they had soon obeyed when Blayze had nipped out to help the situation.

With the ship now as barren as a ghost town, Blayze took the controls and asked Simon to keep a watchful eye on the screens. Moving each camera one by one, they noticed that there were many areas of the ship that the camera simply couldn't see.

"Wait!" Simon shouted. "I just saw something move." Trying to remember which screen it was, Simon knew it was one just to his left. "There," he pointed. "Did you see that?" he asked Blayze without taking his eyes off the screen.

"What number is that?" Blayze asked.

"Camera 21. It looks like the casino, I think."

"Got it. Hang on." Blayze found the correct camera and moved it.

"Go right," Simon directed. "Can you zoom in? There's something just beyond those tables."

As the camera zoomed, Blayze looked eager to see what Simon had seen. There he was. David was standing at the far end of the casino, near a crew door. "Is he..." Blayze zoomed in closer. "...waving? The little fucker is waving at us! He knows we are watching him." They both looked as David stuck his middle finger up and exited through the crew door. "Where does that door lead to?" Blayze asked Simon.

"I've never been through that one, so I don't know."

"Great. Lost him already." Blayze pushed his seat back in anger.

"He'll reappear, don't worry." Although Simon was still angry and upset with everything that had happened, he was determined to find David and stop him.

They continued to look at the different screens in front of them, Blayze moving cameras left to right, hoping for a glimpse. "Got you, you little shit!" Blayze zoomed his camera in.

"What's he doing?" Simon asked.

"Trying to make us look stupid, that's what he doing." They watched as David helped himself to a drink behind the bar on the Lido deck. Saying nothing, they continued to stare at the screen as David took a seat on a sun lounger and sipped his drink. "He's mine. Let's go."

Dashing out of the security office on Deck 5, Blayze lead the way up the stairs. Simon followed, noticing how fast Blayze could run. Being a dancer, Simon thought he was fitter than most, but this guy was quick. They had just reached the top of the stairs, arriving on Deck 8, when they were confronted by a female passenger. She noticed Simon's badge as they tried to get past.

"You, sir! I want a word with you, now!" she said, stepping in front of Simon and waving her finger. She was in her mid-to-late sixties, Simon reckoned, and she didn't look thrilled.

"I'll deal with this," Simon said, looking at Blayze. "You carry on."

"'This'?" she butted in. "Young man. 'This' has a name!"

Blayze glanced at the lady and then back at Simon. "Good luck," he mouthed, and continued up the stairs.

LEAVING SIMON DOWN on Deck 8, Blayze only had a few flights of stairs to climb before he reached the Lido deck. He slowed down, so as not to scare David away. He tried to remember what he had seen on the screen to deduce exactly where on the deck David was sitting.

As he approached, the sensor opened the glass double doors in front of him. He crept out, passing the bar that David had been behind. He slowly walked further onto the open deck and noticed a drink on a table between two sun loungers, which were facing away from him. He needed the element of surprise, so didn't say a word and took a few extra steps closer.

Suddenly, music blasted out at full volume behind him, deafening him. Startled, he turned around to see an empty stage, with no one at the controls. As he turned back around to the sun loungers, he noticed David starting to run. Blayze chased him, but David had a head start and was already almost at the exit, at the other end of the deck. Continuing in pursuit, Blayze ran as fast as he could, but by the time he had reached the spot where David had just been, he had gone.

Frantically searching around, Blayze was faced with stairs leading up and down on both sides. He opted for the stairs to his left and headed down, peering over the banister to see if he could spot any movement.

There was nothing. David had slipped through his fingers.

Pausing on the stairs, Blayze slammed his hands down on the banister. "Fuck!"

Realising he had no alternative, Blayze headed back the same way he had come. Once on the Lido deck, he walked straight to the stage, where the music was still blaring out. He jumped up and noticed that the music had been controlled remotely. Just as he was about to turn off the power, the music changed.

Blayze spun around, now realising he was being watched. He looked everywhere, across both the deck he was on and the one above, which overlooked the Lido deck. He couldn't see anyone, but he knew David was out there, teasing him.

Turning back, Blayze grabbed the lead to the sound system and ripped it from the wall. "Change it now, you little fucker!" he shouted, as he turned to look around one more time. He still couldn't see anyone, so went back to where he had left Simon, needing to get back to the cameras again. He was determined to catch David, and was furious that he had been so close, but had ended up giving David more time.

CHAPTER SEVENTEEN

Simon walked the passenger who had stopped him back towards her cabin, but she refused to go in until he gave her some answers.

"Until you tell me exactly what is going on, you are not going anywhere. We're being locked in our cabin for no reason. Like prisoners!"

"Madam, it's for your own safety," Simon said for the third time.

"You wouldn't know safety if it hit you between the eyes! We are starving and thirsty in here, and my husband cannot last on just peanut butter and jelly sandwiches all night." She put both hands on her hips and stared at Simon.

"I'll see if I can get you something different," Simon offered. He attempted to walk away but was stopped by her grabbing his arm.

"What I want is to be let out, so I can choose my own food, thank you very much. We've paid enough to be here."

Simon pulled his arm away and stopped her. "I know you have, madam, and so has everyone else. You don't see them complaining about it, do you?" He pointed down the empty hallway. "Once the virus is under control, you will be allowed to leave your cabin and eat as much as you want. Now will you just get inside?" Simon was becoming more and more frustrated, and his tone had gone from kind to harsh. He just wanted to leave.

"I will report this. You can't talk to me like that."

He forced his name tag in front of her face, so she could get a good look. He wasn't bothered about any report; he had more pressing matters to deal with. "Simon, England, Dance Captain. You got that?"

She turned away and opened her door. "How rude," she uttered as she went into her cabin. Simon watched as she picked up a pen and piece of paper and he took the opportunity to get away. He was already at the end of the corridor when he heard her shout, "Come back here, I'm not finished with you yet!"

But the hand on his back stopped him from returning.

BLAYZE HAD JUST MADE his way down onto Deck 8 when he heard a woman's voice. He walked around the corner to see where it was coming from and noticed her facing away from him. "Excuse me, ma'am," he said while walking towards her. "Are you the lady that Simon was helping?"

She turned to face him and dropped her pen and paper to her side. "Well, if you call that help. He just walked away from me. You might be able to help me, though. Do you work here?"

"No, ma'am, I'm just helping them out. How long ago did he leave?" Blayze asked, wondering where Simon would have gone to.

"How come you're allowed out and we aren't? If you're allowed to roam the ship, then so can we!"

Blayze took out his phone and tried to call Simon, but there was no answer. "How long ago did he leave?" he asked again.

"I don't know what you want with that rude man, anyway. Walking away from me — who does he think he is?"

Time was of the essence and Blayze still needed to find David. "Listen. Tell me what happened and then get back in your cabin until we say so, or I will arrest you for wasting my time," he snapped. This woman was doing his head in.

"Well, if you put it like that. He went that way just a few moments before you arrived." She pointed in the direction she had been facing when he had first seen her.

Blayze started heading that way. "Thank you."

"He was with someone else when he left," she added. Blayze stopped.

"Who?"

"How am I supposed to know?" she shrugged. "Jeans and a white T-shirt, that's all I could see from here."

"Get back inside," Blayze replied, "and lock your door." He turned to rush after Simon, who he knew was with David.

As Blayze sprinted down the hallway, he could hear the woman talking to her husband. "There's something else going on here that they aren't telling us."

SIMON WAS BEING SHOVED from behind, each push forcing him down the stairs near the front of the ship. "Where are we going?" he asked.

"Just keep your mouth shut and get moving," ordered David, giving him another push.

"It doesn't have to be this way."

David shoved him again, throwing him against the wall on the landing. "I said shut up! What part of that don't you get?" Simon's back hit a ridge on the wall and he winced in pain. "You think that's painful? Just you wait."

He pulled Simon off the wall and forced him to continue down the stairs. "Get in," he ordered as they reached the backstage entrance. Simon opened the door and went through. "Down that way," David pointed. Simon followed his instructions.

They reached a storage room close to the stage. It was filled with scenery from the various shows they did, all tied up against the walls. The room also stored spare lighting, rigging equipment, and anything else the crew needed. David followed Simon in, grabbing a microphone lead from a box while passing.

He pointed to a large pole near the edge of the room. "Stand there and wrap your arms around it," he ordered. Simon did as he was told. He had no intention of dying. David wrapped the lead around Simon's wrists, tying him to the post.

"Why are you doing this?" Simon asked while David searched the room for anything else he could use.

"Why? Why? I'll tell you why." David stopped his search and walked directly towards Simon, standing so close that Simon could feel his breath on his face. "She fucking lied to me for years and put me through hell!"

"Who did?"

"Rachel did. Do you know what it's like to be told your baby is dead? Well, do you?!" David shouted in Simon's face. Simon pulled back as far as he could, shaking his head in fear. "I knew she was pregnant before she left the ship. We had a row on our last night and she told me. She left the next day without saying a word and then I was told, by her mother, of all people, that she had an abortion without asking me. She killed my baby!"

"I'm so sorry," Simon said, attempting to comfort him.

"I don't need your pity. I don't need anyone's pity. I fell into a deep depression after finding that news out and it took me over two years to get over it. Then I saw her again, on here. I knew it would be tough, and I tried so hard."

David perched on the edge of one of the scenery pieces in front of Simon. "We argued a couple of times over the last few months, over insignificant things that I admit I shouldn't have brought up. It wasn't until this week that she sent me over the edge. Finding out your baby is still alive after this long came as a huge shock. I had suffered for two years, and for what? For her to keep my baby from me? I don't think so."

"That's awful. How could she?" Simon said, still scared but wanting David to feel like he was on his side.

"One day, I called her up and said that I wanted to see my child. She refused and said that she didn't want me anywhere near her. That was the first time I heard I had a daughter. A fucking daughter. You know what, Simon?" He stood back up and walked over to Simon again. "I was willing to forget the past, forget what she had done, so that I could have a life with my daughter in it. But oh no, she wasn't going to give me that. So we fought and screamed at each other over the phone." Simon just listened, not wanting to say any more, as he could see David getting angrier and angrier the more he recalled what had happened. "You know what she said then?" Simon shook his head. "She said, 'she's not yours anyway, so you can fuck off'. Not mine? We were together for the six months before she was pregnant. How could the baby not be mine?" He started pacing around the room with pent up anger.

"What happened, David?" Simon questioned.

"Well, I cried. Then I cried some more. And then the sadness turned into rage and anger. I wanted to know who the father was. It didn't take long to find out." He started to walk slowly around Simon. "Funny how much information people will tell you when their life is being dangled over the side of a ship, isn't it?" he whispered in Simon's ear, making him cower. "The captain knew the baby was his all along. Rachel had been hiding her away from everyone, pretending it was her sister's until the day she was to leave the ships. The captain had promised to leave his family for her, like they always do, but I knew he wouldn't." He walked back round to face Simon. "The feeling of throwing him overboard was delightful." The glint Simon saw in David's eyes when he said that was frightening. He was now stuck in a room with a cold-hearted killer who enjoyed what he had done.

"And Rachel? What happened with her?" Simon asked out of curiosity, wanting to know if David killed her.

"Well, when I told her what I'd done, and that I knew everything, she went ballistic and threatened to have me arrested. Now, I couldn't let that happen, could I? A young girl jumps overboard after a lovers' quarrel, that's what it was meant to look like. Unlucky for me, she was rescued. Otherwise that would have been the end."

"And everyone else? Alice, Tammy, Robert, and now Andrew. You killed them all too?"

"They were asking too many questions, and I knew at some point they would figure it all out. I wasn't prepared for that to happen. So they had to go."

"And me?" Simon asked, knowing that David had just told him everything. Everyone else who had found out just one detail was already dead.

"Your fate has been sealed, mate."

David grabbed a roll of black masking tape from the shelf near Simon's head and put a piece over his mouth. "Right, no more questions." He tied some around Simon's legs, either side of the pole, making sure he couldn't go anywhere. "I'll be back for you soon," he whispered in Simon's ear. Simon tried to wriggle, but he was stuck. David reached the door and turned around. Simon stared right at him as he just winked and closed the door behind him, turning the light off as he left. Tears started to run down Simon's cheeks as he was left bound and gagged in the darkness with no one knowing where he was.

BLAYZE HAD GONE BACK to the security office and had been joined by Ananda, who was helping to look for signs of David and Simon. Knowing Simon was now in immediate danger, they had to search quickly. Blayze had called Antonio to update him on what had happened and asked him to make another announcement, this one telling everyone to lock their doors. Even though he knew it would alarm people, he couldn't take the risk of anyone else being hurt. Antonio had agreed and made the announcement.

They were now only a few hours from Miami, so Blayze called his office to send backup right away. He had updated them on the situation at hand and explained that there was now a potential hostage situation. "Help's on its way," he told Ananda, who was still looking at the screen in front of them for any sign of movement.

"How long will they be?" Ananda asked.

"The coastguard are sending a chopper and having some local police join them."

"I'll have some of my guys on deck, ready to meet them."

"We need to find David first, though, so we know where to send them." They continued to stare at the screens, but nothing was happening. Blayze pushed his chair back and stood up. "I can't sit here all day. Ananda, you stay here and watch out, and radio me if you see anything." Blayze grabbed a radio from the table and headed towards the door.

"What are you going to do?"

"I'm going to hunt for the little fucker. He ain't getting away from me again." Blayze left, slamming the door behind him.

Blayze made his way to the front of the ship, into the theatre, and looked around the auditorium. There weren't any signs of movement, so he left and headed towards the shopping mall. Everywhere he went, he looked left to right, up and down, but he couldn't see anything. He peered in the piano bar. Nothing.

Moving along the deck, past the coffee shop, he reached the sports bar and noticed the TV behind the bar was still on. As he watched the CNN news broadcast, it showed a helicopter circling a cruise ship. Upon closer inspection, he realised it was the Majestic Dream. The ship he was on. "What the hell?" he said to himself, moving over to a nearby window and spotting the helicopter. He went back over to the TV, grabbed the remote and turned up the volume. He needed to hear exactly what was being said.

"Headline News: A cruise ship, just off the coast of Miami, has a missing captain and four unexplained deaths. Sources say that the ship is on lockdown because of Norovirus, yet reports of a man being chased have been sighted."

"How the hell have they got hold of this?" Blayze perched on a stool to hear the rest.

"Two of the deaths occurred in Antigua," the newscaster continued. "The victims have not yet been named but are both female."

'Oh, fuck,' Blayze thought. 'Anyone on here watching this is going to know they're talking about this ship.' His phone rang.

"Are you seeing this?" asked Antonio.

"If you're talking about the news, I've just caught it, yes."

"Where are they getting their information from?"

"I don't know, but it's someone on board, that's for sure. I'm currently searching for David, and Ananda is in his office, keeping an eye on the cameras."

"I'm heading to the bridge for the arrival of the coastguard. Keep me posted."

"Will do." Blayze hung up. He continued his search along that deck and reached the dining room. He wandered through the tables and chairs and stood in the middle of the room to look around. Still no sign of anyone. Making his way back along the same deck, towards the centre of the ship, he passed the TV again.

"What the fuck?!" On the screen was a picture of him standing in the dining room, where he had just been, with his full name and position beside the image. He was being followed. His phone started ringing off the hook as everyone who had his number wanted to know what was going on. He didn't answer any of the calls, instead switching his phone onto silent. Knowing he was being followed, he realised he could turn this to his advantage and lead whoever it was out into the open. He knew that the best place to do this was on the Lido deck, as there he would be quick enough to spot them before they managed to run away.

He headed up the stairs and made his way outside. He passed the large, empty pool, making his way across the deck between the deserted sun loungers. Suddenly he spun around and spotted a young man holding up his phone. "Who the hell are you?" Blayze shouted across the open deck.

"I'm a journalist for the Miami Herald. Paul's the name," the man yelled back as Blayze walked towards him.

"So, it's you who has leaked all of this information, is it?"

"Well, there's definitely a story going on here. Didn't take a lot of digging to get people to talk. After seeing you search the ship with officers on board and then hearing your name, I knew something was wrong. I recognised you from the news last week. All I had to do was say I was you, and people opened up over the phone. Can I get a comment?"

Blayze pushed angrily past him. "What you have done may have cost the life of another crew member! If they die, their blood is on your hands." Blayze snatched the man's phone and threw it over the side of the ship. "Report that, you fucking idiot."

AS BLAYZE MADE HIS way down the stairs, he met a group of the ship's security guards who were on their way up. "Special Agent Carlson, the coastguard are almost here," one of them declared. Blayze wanted to be the first to brief them all, so he tagged along with the security guards. They made their way towards the helicopter pad on the highest deck of the ship, just aft of the ship's funnel.

They stood on the steps of the deck while they saw the helicopter approach, not wanting to get in the way. The helicopter circled the ship once, then came back around and landed safely. Not waiting for the propellers to stop, the coastguard and the police jumped out and met Blayze and the security guards on the steps. "Follow me," Blayze said, and he lead them towards the bridge.

A policeman took off his headgear and introduced himself. "I'm Lieutenant Fernandez from the Miami Police Department."

"Glad to have you on board." Blayze shook his hand. "Blayze Carlson, FBI." He gestured to Antonio, who had met them as they arrived. "This is Antonio, acting captain."

"So, we have ourselves a serial killer on board, do we?" asked Lieutenant Fernandez, shaking Antonio's hand. "And what's the hostage's name?"

"Simon Hutchins. He's the dance captain on board and has been helping us out with our efforts to catch David," Blayze answered.

"And got himself caught, instead," Antonio added.

"Listen, guys, this man has hurt enough people already," Blayze started. "I won't let him hurt any more. We will use the bridge as our command centre. Ananda, the chief security officer, is in his office on Deck 5, keeping a close eye on all the security cameras on board. He will update us if he sees anything."

"How much do we know of this man, David?" the lieutenant asked.

Blayze stepped forward to address everyone. They all turned to face him to give their undivided attention. "Our suspect is David Pennington, thirty-five years old. He is a white male, six feet tall, with long dark hair and a British accent. He has a recent history of depression and stopped taking his medication a few months ago. He is an angry, volatile man who is impulsive and easily triggered. He has now killed five members of his own department, with another one, as far as we are aware, still alive and being held hostage. As for the captain, we are still investigating his whereabouts. The suspect knows this ship inside and out, so we need to have our eyes open at all times." Blayze walked over to a map of the ship that was on the nearby wall and pointed out a position for all to see. "He was last seen here on Deck 8 walking towards the front of the ship by a passenger who informed us that he was wearing a pair of jeans and a white T-shirt. It is the same outfit that I saw him in while pursuing him a moment before he took Simon Hutchins hostage."

Lieutenant Fernandez stepped forward to join Blayze. "Okay, guys, let's spread out and find our man," he ordered. His team exited the bridge, along with Blayze, to begin their sweep of the ship, leaving the coastguard on the bridge with Antonio, who had to get them to Miami as fast as possible.

Blayze passed Antonio, who was now at the door, waiting for them all to leave. "Whatever you do, don't let anyone in here until this is all over."

CHAPTER EIGHTEEN

David had crept his way up onto the open deck and had witnessed the arrival of the helicopter. He had seen how many officers had got off and knew that they would all be looking for him right away. He stood up and waved towards the helicopter. "I'm over here," he shouted. The sound of the blades still spinning had muffled his call, and he watched them all walk away from him. "Hide and seek should be much more interesting now," he muttered to himself as he headed back down the stairs.

He reached the theatre and headed towards the storage room where he had left Simon tied up in the dark. Bursting through the door, he switched the light on and noticed Simon's reaction went from relief to dread as he dropped his head. "Too bright for you?" he asked as he walked over and slapped Simon twice on the cheek. "It's only me." He grabbed Simon's hair and pulled his head back up. "I know I'm leaving the ship in handcuffs or a body-bag. Either way, there's no escaping this now. May as well go out with a bang, right?"

SIMON WAS SWEATING with nerves and his eyes were red from the tears that had poured while being in there all alone. As David let go of his hair, Simon started shaking his head, trying to speak from behind the tape covering his mouth. He kept mumbling until David finally ripped the tape off. "You don't have to do this," Simon pleaded. "Please." But there was no getting through to him. Everything he tried to say just fell on deaf ears.

"Honestly, you don't half whine for a grown man," David said, pulling a large coil of rope out of a box he found at the bottom of the shelves attached to the wall. "This will do nicely."

Simon realised that the rope was for him and fell silent. He watched as David rummaged through more boxes, collecting tape and screwdrivers before dumping them all at Simon's feet. "Please, David, I've done nothing wrong! We were friends!"

David laughed out loud. "Friends? Who are you kidding? I had to lie next door and listen to you screw Rachel one night, not that long ago. Remember?"

Simon looked away in shock, knowing that he hadn't told anyone about it. "We were drunk, and it was just one night. How did you know?" Simon asked inquisitively.

"I dated her, remember? I would recognise that orgasm anywhere. I knew it was her. She knew what I was going through and she had to rub it in my face by doing it right next door. And with you!" David thrust his finger right into Simon's chest. "Fucking another man is one thing, but fucking a gay man. Well, that's just rubbing salt into an open wound."

"Like I said, it was one night. It meant nothing."

"Nothing to you, maybe, but to me it was just another blow."

Simon realised that one drunken night of stupidity could soon cost him his life. He looked down and watched David cut off the tape around his legs. Not thinking, as soon as David stood up, Simon grabbed onto the pole with his forearms as tight as he could and wrapped his legs around David, forcing him into the pole.

It wasn't to last long, though. He had failed to trap one of David's arms. He punched Simon as hard as he could and as he released his grip, David bent down, picked up a screwdriver, and stabbed him in the side. Simon cried in pain and slumped onto the pole, unable to stop the bleeding.

"That's what you get for being fucking stupid." David grabbed the tape off the floor and forced another piece over Simon's mouth. Blood was pouring out from Simon's wound, but David didn't seem to care as he rammed the screwdriver up in Simon's face. "Try anything like that again and the next blow will be to your throat. Got it?"

Unable to speak, Simon just nodded in reply.

David waved the screwdriver in Simon's face. "You've just made my plan much easier, now, thank you."

Simon looked on in horror as David started feeding the rope around the metal girders on the ceiling to create a noose. Once finished, he wrapped the rope around Simon's neck and tightened it, making sure it could not slip off. Simon was trying to speak, but couldn't. He could feel the rope becoming tighter the more he tried to wriggle. David walked back over to the other side of the room where the rope was dangling and pulled it tight. He tied it off on a hook that was attached to the wall.

Slowly making his way back over to Simon, he leaned in and whispered in his ear. "I thought about doing this to myself many times over, years ago, but it looks so much better on someone else." The tears had already started to stream down Simon's face again. David placed a small box at Simon's feet. "Get on," he ordered.

Simon was reluctant to move at first. He knew what it was for. But it didn't take long for David to persuade him; an incision of the screwdriver in his opposite side did the trick. Simon winced in pain again. Now bleeding out from two puncture-holes, one on either side of his body, Simon stood on the box, trembling.

David pulled the rope tighter. "Any last words?"

THE SEARCH HAD BEEN underway for some time and they had covered almost all of the ship, but there was still no sign of David or Simon. Blayze had received a call from Ananda, telling him he thought he may have seen some movement in the forward crew stairwell. Blayze decided to check it out for himself, letting the police officers continue where they were. He was already on Deck 6, roughly halfway between the centre and the front of the ship, so stopped what he was doing and headed straight there.

He ran to the top of the forward crew stairwell to see where it lead. As he opened the door, he could see the coastguard's helicopter blades sticking out from behind the ship's funnel. 'It must have been David that Ananda saw,' he thought, 'and now he knows the police are here!' Blayze knew that David would now be on edge and would react accordingly, potentially costing Simon his life. He shut the door and turned back down the steps. There was nothing but walls and stairs for a few flights with nowhere to check, and then the entrance to backstage appeared. They had checked back there earlier, but something told him it was worth searching there again.

Blayze opened the door and walked down the hallway to the left. He came across one of the dressing rooms and entered. He searched around the costumes that were hung up in the middle of the room, but there was no one in there. He returned the same way he came as he knew there was another dressing room on the opposite side. He searched that one too, and there was still no sign of anyone.

He walked out and went straight ahead, onto the stage. The main curtains were down. He remembered that they hadn't been when they had searched earlier, so he knew that someone must have been up there recently. There wasn't much light. Unable to see easily, and becoming more desperate in his hunt, he stumbled into something covered with a black cloth. He lifted it up to discover it was just a large prop for one of the shows, which he had not seen because of everything that had been going on. All he had wanted was to relax and enjoy his vacation.

He looked around as well as he could, but all he could hear was the sound of metal hitting metal coming from the rig above him. With the ship still moving up and down due to the ocean swells caused by the remnants of the hurricane, anything that hadn't been properly fastened was being shunted around.

Not wanting to end up being crushed by a gigantic metal frame that hung forty foot above him, he swiftly finished his search there and headed down the ramp, leaving via the opposite exit to which he had entered. As he approached the stairs at the centre of the hallway, he noticed a silver door handle on a large black door at the end of the ramp. He looked to his other side and saw the same thing. "How did I miss those?" he asked himself. He headed in the direction he was facing, which was the side of the stage he had originally gone up. He reached the door and gripped the handle, pausing for a second to take in a deep breath. If David was behind the door, he knew he would have to be ready for anything. He pushed the handle down and opened the door.

The door was heavy, and as he opened it fully, it clicked into place. He felt the side of the wall and found the light switch. Illuminating the room, he was presented with a space filled with an array of stage scenery parts. "So this is where they store everything." There were two stacks of tables in the corner strapped to the wall next to shelves of lighting equipment and spare parts. But still no sign of David or Simon.

He left the room and headed towards the equivalent door on the other side. He pushed the silver handle down, but it wouldn't open. Something was jamming it closed. He tried to force it, but it wouldn't budge. He pushed with all of his might but only managed to open it just enough to see that the light was already on.

"Hello? Is anyone in there?" he shouted, but no answer came. He figured that the storm had moved objects behind the door, blocking it. Knowing he would need more force than just himself to get it open, he left to gather more people to help.

SIMON'S ATTACKER WAS standing behind him with his hand over the tape on his mouth, making sure he didn't make a sound. He also had a screwdriver pressing in his back to ensure he didn't try anything stupid. Not wanting to be stabbed again, Simon didn't move a muscle. Once they heard Blayze disappear, David released his grip on Simon and started rushing around the room, knowing he didn't have much time before Blayze would return. Simon watched on as David moved the objects he had placed behind the door which had kept it shut and rigged another piece of rope to the handle on the inside. He then wrapped the other end around the box under Simon's feet. Simon realised then that as soon as the door would be open fully, it would pull the box away, causing him to swing from the ceiling.

Simon couldn't believe what he was seeing. He didn't realise how cunning David really was. He wondered if this is how he had planned his own hanging all those years ago, making it look like it was someone else's fault. A way to pass the blame. All Simon wished now was for Blayze to hurry back and save him from this utter psychopath.

He watched as David walked back towards the rope that was tied to a hook on the wall. He unravelled it slightly, which gave Simon a brief release, but that was to be short-lived. With a huge yank, David raised him higher into the air, until he was on his tiptoes. The strain on his neck was immense. He could feel the blood rushing around his head and he struggled to breathe.

"Comfy up there?" David asked. "Well, I suppose not, but hey, at least it will be a quick — ish — death."

Simon couldn't speak, but raised his middle finger at David.

"Well, that's not very nice, is it? For that one finger, I'll give an extra one." He walked behind Simon, out of his eyesight, and stabbed him once again, this time just under his right shoulder blade. Simon winced again. As his body moved with the motion of the stabbing, it caused the rope to squeeze his neck even harder. He could feel his bones being pulled and knew that if he dropped now, it would all be over. "Well, let's hope he comes back soon and finishes you off before you bleed out everywhere."

Leaving Simon hanging with blood pouring out of his stab wounds, David left the room and turned the light off. Not knowing how long he would be there for, Simon tried his best not to move, but his legs were beginning to struggle.

CHAPTER NINETEEN

B layze reached the policemen, who were now just a few hundred yards from the theatre. "Lieutenant, I think I know where they are. We need to evacuate this entire section of the ship from top to bottom and block it all off so the suspect has nowhere to run."

"Where are they?"

"In a side room, backstage. The door is jammed shut and my suspicion is that David has barricaded the door and knows that we are aware of his location. There are too many exits in this area through which he could escape, so the fewer people around, the better."

"Agreed." Lieutenant Fernandez dispatched his team, ordering them towards various directions to evacuate all passengers in the vicinity of the theatre.

Blayze called Ananda and asked him to get his team to do the same in the crew area, to close off any doors, and to keep guard. "We know where he is, so meet me outside the auditorium." Blayze hung up and helped to usher the people passing by out of the way. Once everybody had been moved out of the area, Lieutenant Fernandez ordered his men to block off all entrances and exits to the front and back of the stage.

Blayze ignored questions from passengers who passed by. Instead, he politely told them to move along to the atrium, where they should be safe. The sight of armed men caused a few people to scream in panic while they were chased down the hallway. Some of the crew, including the remaining cast members and musicians, had also been evacuated and made their way upstairs. Two of the dancers spotted Blayze and headed straight for him.

"What's going on?" John asked. Laura held John's hand for comfort and stuck close to him, scared at the surrounding scene, while others had made their way towards to atrium. "Why have we been evacuated?"

"And you are?" Blayze questioned, not seeing their name tags as he was too busy trying to clear the area.

"We are dancers, on board," John answered.

"Sorry. I didn't recognise you." Remembering that these guys were part of Simon's team and were his friends, Blayze felt he had to tell them the truth. "We have a potential hostage situation backstage. Simon has been taken."

"What?!" John shouted. "Who's taken him?" Laura put her hand over her mouth in shock.

Blayze moved them both over to one side so that other passers-by couldn't hear. "Well, you will not like this, but it's David, your musical director. He's our murderer."

"It can't be," said Laura. "He's not like that all."

"I have to beg to differ. You wouldn't be saying that if you had seen Andrew earlier."

"Wait, what?" The shock in Laura's voice told Blayze that they hadn't been informed of the news. "Andrew's dead?" she asked. The look Blayze gave her answered her question, and she burst into tears in John's arms.

"Listen, guys, you really need to move away from here. We need to go in." Blayze ushered them backwards to go and stand with everyone else.

When Ananda arrived, there were people everywhere, and he had to push past them to get to Blayze. "So where is he?" he asked.

"Starboard side storage room, next to the stage. We need to approach with caution. We don't know what the situation is behind the door."

Lieutenant Fernandez joined them. "You ready?" he asked Blayze.

"Always. Let's do this."

They made their way into the theatre and crept along the edge of the auditorium. Not making a sound, they reached the front of the stage and climbed up one by one. Ananda had already explained that he knew of a little key-pad that was attached to the proscenium arch, which had buttons to play music and also to raise and lower the curtain. He pressed it, and they all stood back and watched the curtain rise. They anxiously waited until it hit the top before moving on, in case of any surprises. Being able to see a lot more than he could the last time he was on the stage, Blayze was able to lead them directly to the door in question.

Lieutenant Fernandez instructed them both to stand behind him. He pulled out his weapon and placed his free palm on the door handle. "Ready?" he said, looking back at Blayze and Ananda. They responded with a nod. Lieutenant Fernandez pushed the handle down to see if the door was still stuck, and, satisfied that it wasn't, threw it open with his full force.

Lieutenant Fernandez went flying in, followed by Blayze and Ananda. The door appeared to have pulled a box away from under Simon's legs and his body had dropped, dangling in the air from the rope attached to his neck. Blayze could not believe the state Simon was in. The amount of blood all over the floor looked like he had been tortured. Simon's body shook as Blayze dashed towards him to get hold of his legs and support his weight.

"Hurry, Ananda, get that rope down!" Blayze shouted.

Ananda followed the rope to where it was attached and released it. Simon struggled to breathe and blood poured all over Blayze's body as he tried to hold on to him.

Lieutenant Fernandez searched the room for signs of David, but he was nowhere to be seen. "He's not here, guys. But he must be close." He rushed over to help catch Simon's body as the rope released. "Let's carry him to the stage so we have more room. Quick!"

"I'll call a medic," Ananda announced, reaching for his phone.

As they placed his body on the black wooden floor, Simon was hardly breathing. Blayze ripped the tape from Simon's mouth and tore his top open to find out where the blood was coming from. When he rolled him over he witnessed an array of puncture wounds. "We need the medic fast, he's losing a lot of blood." Blayze looked up towards the entrance of the theatre and noticed people watching on while Simon lay there, fighting for his life.

AFTER LEAVING SIMON hanging earlier, David had gone to hide backstage. He didn't want to go far as he had wanted to see this death through to the end. He hid in the darkness behind two huge scenery pieces he had found, giving him an excellent view of the doorway.

He had waited patiently and watched Blayze, Ananda and a cop storm into the room, hurrying to try to save Simon. As the three of them crowded around his body on the stage, trying to stop the bleeding and get Simon to breathe again, they had no idea they were being watched from just a few feet away. David unravelled the ropes that were holding an enormous set piece to the ship and, with a big push, he shoved one of them in the direction of Simon's body.

"Guys, watch out!" screamed a voice from the back of the auditorium.

David noticed Blayze lift his head to see who was shouting and then turn to see the set piece hurtling towards them.

"Watch out!" Blayze shouted, but it was too late. It hit Ananda and Lieutenant Fernandez head on, knocking them both to the ground. Having missed his target, David sent another piece flying their way.

BLAYZE DARTED UP AND diverted the set piece away from Simon and, as he did so, he noticed David standing in the wings. They both ran straight for each other and collided on the stage, ending up on the floor. David's fists started flying as he pinned Blayze to the floor. Blayze thrust his hips up and threw David to one side, giving him a chance to roll over and crawl towards him. As he got close, David kicked his leg, smacking Blayze directly in the face and knocking him down.

Lieutenant Fernandez was just coming around from being hit in the side of the head by the set piece and noticed the fight going on to his left. He got on his radio for backup, then leaned over to make sure Ananda was okay. He noticed blood running down Ananda's face, where the set piece had struck him. Simon was still lying there, bleeding, but they had to get hold of David.

DAVID HAD NOTICED THAT the policeman's gun had been left on the floor when they had put Simon's body down, and during the collision, it had been pushed away from him. He got up and rushed towards it but the cop was able to grab his leg as he passed, tripping him up and making him fly forward. Fortunately for David, this was the direction he needed to go and, as he fell forward, onto the ground, he landed on the gun itself. As David turned onto his back, Blayze dived on him, with the gun now between them. They rolled around the floor in a struggle for the gun until David pulled the trigger.

Both of them paused for a second, not knowing if one of them had been shot. Once they had realised they were okay, the struggle continued. David leaned up and headbutted Blayze in the face, sending him ever so slightly backwards. As he lifted the gun up from his chest, Blayze grabbed him by the wrists and forced both hands over his head. Blayze slammed his hands down on the stage floor three times, which released the gun from David's grip. As David looked to either side, he could see more policemen running towards them from all directions. They surrounded him and pointed their guns directly at his face.

David was outnumbered and had no alternative but to stop fighting and surrender. As Blayze moved away, other officers dived in, rolling him over and placing him in handcuffs.

"You're under arrest," Blayze said. "You're going away for a very long time."

"BLAYZE," ANANDA SHOUTED. "We've got a problem."

Wiping himself down, Blayze headed over to Ananda, who was kneeling by Simon's side. "Is he okay?"

"You can add being shot to the list of injuries."

Blayze looked down to see that when the gun had gone off, it had shot Simon in the upper thigh. Blood was now oozing out all over the stage where Simon lay. Blayze jumped in to assist and put as much pressure as he could on Simon's fresh wound. "This isn't good. We need to get him to the infirmary, stat."

When the medical team arrived, Blayze and Ananda lifted Simon's body and took him to the front of the stage, placing him on a stretcher. "He's lost a hell of a lot of blood," Blayze told the doctor. "Multiple stab wounds and a gunshot to the upper thigh."

"Get him downstairs, now," the doctor ordered his staff. He turned back to Blayze. "He's not looking good. I can tell you that already."

Blayze and Ananda followed the medical team to the auditorium doors and were followed by the police, who were escorting David to the brig. As they passed Blayze, David was met by a furious crowd. They shouted abusive comments at him and spat on him as the police officers dragged him along the corridor towards the staircase.

Lieutenant Fernandez came up behind Blayze. "Well done, sir. We got our man."

Blayze shook his hand and thanked him before he joined his men and Ananda. They escorted David down the stairs. Blayze wasn't going to let him out of his sight until he knew he was locked away.

"I need to let Antonio know that we have caught him," Blayze told Ananda. "And update him on Simon's condition."

"I'll inform everyone that it's safe to return to their cabins and that it's all over."

"Excellent idea."

It wasn't long before they reached the brig. Ananda had hurried in front of everyone to open the door ready, and quickly locked it as soon as they had thrown David in.

"Make sure he is guarded around the clock until we reach Miami," Blayze told the police officers. Turning back to Ananda, Blayze continued. "I'm heading to the medical centre now, to check Simon's status."

"Thanks again, Blayze," Ananda shouted after him.

WHEN BLAYZE REACHED the infirmary, he saw Simon's body being worked on by all the available staff. He rushed over to the doctor. "How is he?"

"He needs surgery ASAP. We just don't have the equipment on board for this sort of thing."

"Leave it with me." Blayze reached into his pocket and pulled out his phone. "Antonio, is the coastguard still here?"

"Yes. Why?"

"We need their helicopter. Now. Simon needs surgery fast, otherwise he ain't gonna make it."

"Get him prepared and I'll tell them to meet you up there, right away."

Blayze turned back to the doctor. "Prepare him for emergency airlift, now." He hurried the doctor along, helping as much as he could.

Blayze opened the door. News of Simon's condition had spread, and it had attracted the attention of many crew members. They had gathered outside the medical centre, all wanting an update. "Guys, you need to make room. We need to get upstairs right away."

The stretcher came flying out of the door, with Simon tightly strapped down. He was hooked up to various machines and drips, but he looked lifeless as he passed by the crew. Some of them burst into tears as soon as they saw him. He was well-known on board, and Blayze imagined it must be hard to see a friend and colleague fighting for his life.

Knowing the helicopter was towards the back of the ship, Blayze hurried along to call down the elevator and kept the door open. As soon as the stretcher arrived, they headed to the open deck.

Outside, the weather had brightened up a little. The rain had eased off, but the wind was still strong, so they kept a tight grip on the stretcher and headed for the helicopter. The pilot had already arrived and had started the engine. The propellers were almost at full speed, ready to go. All they had to do now was to carry Simon up the steps to the helicopter, but they were too narrow to carry the stretcher from either side.

Luckily, some of Simon's team members had run up the stairs to see him off and were watching what was happening. Among them, John, one of the dancers, saw their predicament and rushed in to help. "I'm used to lifting people. Let me help."

Blayze made his way towards Simon's head, which was by the first step. "We need to lift him high and get him over the railing." He looked at the medical staff around him. They were lifesavers, not body builders, and Simon wasn't light.

"Come on, out of the way. I've got this," John said, as he pushed the medical staff out of the way and placed his hands under the stretcher by Simon's feet.

"Ready?" Blayze asked. "On three. One, two, three." With John's help, they lifted Simon up to head height, clearing the railing by several inches. Carefully they made their way up the stairs and, as Blayze got to the top, he lowered the stretcher to the ground, avoiding the spinning blades above them. Once John had placed Simon's feet end down, the medical staff who had followed him up the stairs ushered him aside. John and Blayze stood and watched them put the stretcher into the helicopter and strap Simon up. Two of the medical staff got in with him to ensure his safety during the journey.

Once Blayze and the rest of the remaining medical staff had cleared away, he gave the signal for the pilot to take off.

They stood back as wind rushed upon their faces from the speed of the propellers. They watched as the helicopter lifted off and looped around the front of the ship, heading towards land.

"He'll be alright, won't he?" John asked Blayze.

"I really hope so, mate." Blayze put his hand on John's shoulder and looked back at the helicopter, now off in the distance. "I'll tell you one thing, though. I could do with a drink."

John looked at him and nodded. "Yep. Me too."

Blayze stood aside and opened his arm. "Show me the way."

THE ENTERTAINMENT TEAM, Blayze, Antonio, and Ananda had gathered in the crew bar to raise a toast to the lives lost. They had congregated in the far corner of the bar, away from the other crew members, all with drinks in their hands. Some were chatting about their missing friends, while others were talking about how David had pulled the wool over their eyes and had acted like nothing had happened.

Antonio pulled Blayze and Ananda over to one side. "I'm not going announce this right now, but while you were assisting Simon off the ship, we had word from the coastguard. They informed me that Captain Argenti's body had washed up on the shores of Key West during the storm."

"I'm so sorry," Blayze said, shaking Antonio's hand.

Antonio stepped forward to address everyone. "Can I please have everyone's attention for a moment?" Everyone stopped talking and focussed their attention towards him. "I'd just like to say a huge thank you to Blayze here. Without him, we would never have caught David." He raised his glass. "To Blayze." Everyone raised their glasses and took a sip.

Blayze stepped forward. "You guys came on this ship to work and to enjoy yourselves, yet this week you have been dealt the biggest blow. The past cannot be undone, and we can't bring our loved ones back. All we can do is remember them in our hearts and minds. Remember the good bits, not the bad. How they made you laugh and smile." As he glanced around at everyone, he noticed some smiley faces nodding in agreement, but also some tears from others as they recalled their missed friends. "So let's raise our glasses and remember Rachel, Robert, Alice, Tammy, and Andrew, who are all up there now, looking down on us, wondering why the drinks aren't flowing faster. And telling me that I need to shut up and get a move on." Some chuckles came from around the crowd, along with the odd smile. "Finally, to Simon, who is still with us, but fighting for his life." Blayze raised his glass once more. "To friends."

"To friends," the crowd replied.

Everyone stayed in the bar, and more drinks flowed. People shared various stories they remembered from when they had first met their friends, and, one by one, they all came over to thank Blayze for catching the killer and for saving their lives. The last person he spoke to was John, and Blayze asked him to pass on a message to everyone for him.

Blayze stood and watched them all chat for a while before he said his goodbyes and retired for the night. He had one last job to do.

CHAPTER TWENTY

It was just after dawn, and the ship was pulling into the port of Miami. Blayze was up on the crew deck at the front of the ship, watching them sail in. It was the end of what was meant to have been a relaxing vacation after taking down one of the biggest drug lords he had come across.

The rising sun illuminated Miami's tall glass towers, shining its orange glow on the city below them. It was a glorious sight, and he stood there for a moment to take it all in. As the ship got closer to the cruise terminal, the blue and red lights on the pier side flashed brighter. It was time to get David out of the brig and ready to be moved.

Blayze headed back inside and met Lieutenant Fernandez at the entrance to the brig. "Is the prisoner secure?" Blayze asked.

Lieutenant Fernandez turned to his men, who had been guarding the door all night. "Get the prisoner out," he ordered. They opened the door and brought David towards them. His hands were behind his back, in handcuffs, and he held his head down, trying to avoid looking at anyone. He was still covered in Andrew and Simon's blood, which had stained his white T-shirt. Getting hold of one shoulder each, Blayze and Lieutenant Fernandez walked him to the long corridor which lead to the gangway.

"I have a little surprise for you," Blayze whispered in David's ear. Once they had entered the corridor, David looked up. The entire space in front of him was lined with all of his colleagues in the crew. None of them spoke. They just stared at him.

Blayze and Lieutenant Fernandez gripped David's arms and started slowly walking him past them, all the way along the corridor. As David passed each person, they turned their back to him. The sombre parade seemed to last forever, and David kept his head down until they were about to reach the gangway.

He looked up, and there in front of him were his band members, alongside the rest of the entertainment department. The look of shame and guilt shone across his face as his old friends turned their backs on him, one by one.

"You will remember that for the rest of your life while you rot in jail," Blayze said as he lead him down the gangplank.

Two officers on the pier came over and took David away. Blayze watched as they placed him in the back of the car, and spotted David's vacant expression on his face looking back at the ship as the door closed. Assistant Director Stone had been there to meet Blayze and was waiting by her car. Blayze walked over, his face illuminated by the flashing lights from the police cars.

"So much for a relaxing vacation, hey," Stone remarked. "Do you find trouble or does trouble just find you?"

Blayze shrugged his shoulders and smiled. "Well, as they say, there's no rest for the wicked. Next time, though, I think I'll just relax at home, instead."

"Get your things and I'll give you a ride home. Have you thought about what I asked? I've another case waiting for you, if you want it."

Blayze paused for a second and turned to face the cruise ship behind him. He glanced back over his shoulder. "Bring it on."

EPILOGUE

Six months later, Blayze was standing outside the head office of Paradise Cruises. It was a glorious sunny morning with not a cloud in the sky. The company had erected a memorial for the crew members who had lost their lives during David Pennington's killing spree.

Blayze had brought some flowers, which he laid on the ground by the foot of the enormous stone on which the victims' names had been engraved. He read the plaque above their names. "In Strength, there is Honor. In Courage, there is Valor. In Life, there is Love. In Death, there is Peace. We remember those who fell in September 2019. Always and forever in our hearts."

He looked down at the names below, each with their job title beneath. Rachel Lawson, Dancer, USA. Tammy Harrison, Dancer, USA. Andrew Hinde, Dancer, UK. Alice Shephard, Assistant Cruise Director, UK, and Robert Fairchild, Cruise Director, UK.

"You missed me, then?" said a voice behind him.

Blayze recognised the voice and turned around with open arms. "Simon! So good to see you." They embraced each other with a long hug. "When did you get out of hospital?"

"Oh, I've been out for a few weeks, now." As they parted, they looked back at the memorial. "They offered me a job here at head office."

"That's awesome news."

"Yeah. This way I can come and sit by this stone and talk to my friends when I need to get away from it all."

"How are you holding up?"

"Getting there, day by day. And I'm in touch with all of their families, which is great."

"So you're staying out here, then?"

"Yeah, why not? Beats the British weather. And you guys have better storms."

Blayze chuckled and put his arm around Simon. They looked at the memorial together. "You were a true friend to them all."

"And if it wasn't for you, who knows how many names would be on this? Including mine. You saved my life and I will never forget that." Simon turned to give Blayze another hug. "Listen, I need to head back in, but catch up soon?" Simon started to walk towards the office and Blayze waved.

"Soon, mate. Soon."

From the Author

Thank you for reading Cruise. If you enjoyed it, or even if you didn't, I would love to hear from you. You can contact me either by emailing zakyatesauthor@gmail.com or by finding me on Twitter, where my handle is @zakyatesauthor

For updates on Blayze's next case and other new releases, please feel free to visit my website and subscribe to my mailing list at the link below.
www.zakyates.com

Acknowledgements

This book would not have been possible without the input and support of my wonderful husband, Alex. The numerous edits and proof-readings he did really helped to make this book the best it could be.

Thank you to all my friends and family for their continuous support.

Other books by the Author

The Factory

Now dead, Peter will have to follow everyone he knows to solve the mystery of his own murder. What he discovers along the way is not what he had expected.

Editorial review
"Leaping from one intense scene to the next, this manic story is undeniably dark – boldly touching on issues of abuse, dishonesty, and repressed aggression. Delivering a raw story packed with unapologetic drama, there is a jagged authenticity to the writing that makes this short novella a compelling read."
Self-Publishing Review – 4 Stars

Available from
www.zakyates.com

Printed in Great Britain
by Amazon

83493530R00140